I0650753

Moonlight Visions

Moonlight Visions

tales of

marvel, magic, and mystery

Gary D. Wilson

Haley's

Athol, Massachusetts

© 2023 by Gary Wilson.

All rights reserved. With the exception of short excerpts in a review or critical article, no part of this book may be re-produced by any means, including information storage and retrieval or photocopying equipment, without written permission of the publisher, Haley's.

Haley's
488 South Main Street
Athol, MA 01331
haley.antique@verizon.net • 978.249.9400

Visit garywilsonbooks.net.

Proof read by Richard Bruno.
Cover photo by Frank Aronson.

International Standard Book Number, trade paperback
978-1-948380-84-3

Library of Congress Cataloging-in-Publication Data pending

Contents

It All Began Over a Trip to Israel
a foreword by Cynthia Crosson

It all began over a trip to Israel. I knew Gary Wilson as my parishioner, a church trustee, and our financial guru for the church that I pastor. He was our numbers man, competent at helping us to keep afloat financially. Typical of a small church where relationships develop, I got to know Gary and his wife over my fifteen years as their pastor. Gary knew of my own writing career and had read at least one of my books. He asked if I would like to read some of his writing about his time in the Holy Land.

"I'd love to read something you wrote," I responded. It was a side of Gary I had not seen.

His memoir began with his time in Israel—young, a free spirit living from day to day and experience to experience. It gave me a whole different picture of the Gary I know. His story read more like a journal and, in fact, he said that he had written it for his children and never really thought of publishing it.

When Gary told me that he wanted to keep the account only for his children's eyes, he suggested he had other stories he considered a labor of love. Imagine my surprise when the person I knew as a man of numbers produced a series of whimsical and sometimes dark fables.

Gary began telling me about stories—fables—that came to him in his dreams and begged to be written when he awakened. He paraphrased some of the stories with an excitement that appealed to my writer soul. Would I like to read the stories, he asked?

My own writing has been educational along with several memoirs and a couple of children's books. I have explored fantasy and wondered how I would feel about stories obviously different from my known genres. Gary mentioned that he had shared his stories with several people in our church. They loved what he wrote and encouraged him.

His fables and stories captivated me. He writes of mythical characters perhaps out of fairy tales with complex and often sad problems. I looked forward to the story unfolding as I wondered what the characters would do next. What would Camille make of her good fortune at the price of loss? What new shape would the shapeshifter adopt? Would the ice queen win against her foes? Will the child unravel the riddles for the mythical creatures?

As I read, I was carried to another time, a time of kings and queens, dragons and other mythical creatures, and otherworldly events that challenged my imagination. Part fantasy, part fairy tale—part Gary's imagination.

"Aren't they fun?" a previous reader had asked.

Some stories read grim with a whiff of Stephen King when horrors abound, while other light and fanciful stories end happily.

Gary's stories will take readers from the confines of a living room to whole new worlds far away and sometimes a bit bizarre. Shapeshifters, magic pills, and the keyhole of frightening visions will entertain readers and even sweep them away to the Far East and Africa.

Gary's stories will transport readers in his tales of moonlight visions.

Visions to Captivate

I'll tell you now of some that he wrote, for these stories will unfold
with pen and ink and candlelight, he toils to write tales to be told—
mystery, romance, magic, and lives wrought with destiny or fate,
bringing a tear or a gasp of delight with the words he would create.

Each and every one of them is unique in its own way,
the story that they tell to you and what they have to say.
He hopes that when the tale is told, it will intrigue and stimulate
as he pushes his mind to think beyond for visions to captivate.

The Pearled Seashell
Discovery and a Message Delivered

The story starts in a small hamlet in Wales near by the rocky shores,
in a land of ancient ruins and tales of ghosts, filled with bogs and moors
where locals gather at the taverns to drink, to reminisce once more
of Fairies, Druids, Witches, and Gnomes, in their traditional folklore.

Stories of supernatural spirits as well keep children up at night.
It is all part of the culture that generations share and recite.
So this is where we shall begin, with a young man traversing the shore,
stepping from rock boulder to rock boulder till he stood at the fore

of the cove he visited so often, one of his favorites,
for there he would find his little treasures, pieces of colored glass bits,
as he sifted by hand through the stone pebbles at the base of the sheer cliffs.
That was where waves washed them ashore, those little ocean gifts.

But this day would be different, different from any previous day,
for what he would find would change his life. His past would be cast away.
For some may call it destiny or fate, but who are we to say?
For whatever you want to call it, everything changed that day.

He pulled a piece of glass but found it was a perfect pearled seashell.
He blew the sand off with his lips, and with his sleeve, he wiped it well.
He placed it up and close to his ear and was shocked to hear a voice.
He then pressed it closer to his ear, drawn in as if he'd had no choice.

It was clearly a woman who softly said, in a trembling tone as she spoke,
"I need your help, so I summon you. My request I beseech and invoke."
He replied frantically, saying, "Who is this?" and then,
"Who am I talking to?"
She said, "You'll find me in a cage that's locked,
one woven with rigid bamboo."

"Please tell me where you are," he exclaimed, "for how else can I find you?"
But he could tell her voice was drawing away, and
before it totally withdrew,
she hushed and faintly whispered.
It was the last thing he heard as she spoke.
"You'll know for sure that I'm the one.
I'm the one wearing a mourning cloak."

And then there was only silence as he stood in disbelief,
but her voice had saddened him deeply, for he knew it was filled with grief.
He put the seashell in his pack and made his way back to the town,
then entered the tavern to discuss the unusual object that he had found.

Conversations in the Tavern and His Past Revealed

The others gathered closely around him to hear his impassioned tale
of the woman who spoke through the seashell and her story of travail.
They mumbled and shook their heads,
for they were perplexed and confused
but then started to laugh and grabbed their drinks,
for they were obviously amused.

"You had us going there, boy," they said, and,
"We've heard a lot of tall tales.
You seem so serious about it, too,
but you're missing many pertinent details,

4

like, how can you find this one," they said,
"if you only know her by her voice?"
The young man confidently replied,
"I'll find her, because I have no other choice."

"Yeah, and I'm the King of England," another said, and
they all had a hearty laugh.
An elderly man in the back of the room stood,
perhaps on the young man's behalf,
and every head in the tavern turned his way to listen to what he would say:
"Let me remind everyone who's here tonight
of the boy who had lost his way.

"Remember when he came out of the woods those many years ago?
We asked him where he came from, and his reply was 'I don't know.'
Something had happened to his memory, for it had been taken away,
but we welcomed him in with loving arms to this hamlet by the bay."

To the young man, he said,
"So the whole hamlet basically raised you, for then you were just a teen.
No one bothered you with further questions of where you may have been.
Perhaps this shell and its message are something from your past,
maybe something that shouldn't be ignored but questions only asked.

"I'll conclude with this advice for you, and this is all I'll say.
You'll have to find the Druid first," he said, "for that is the only way."
Then others in the room began to talk about stories they had been told,
that Druids were Celtic lore keepers with an oath sworn to knowledge untold
while others said they're from a mystical order
with no written form to uphold.

Then they ended by saying to the young man, "Go seek if you're so bold!
Best of luck to you, lad, for there's been
no sight of a Druid in a hundred years."
And then everyone in the tavern laughed and
ordered another round of beers.

About to leave the room, the young man rose, discouraged and resigned.
His friends didn't believe him, and doubts began to fill his mind.
He walked and stood on the stony bridge above the stream and felt inclined
to toss the seashell into the water below and leave the mystery behind.

The Search for The Druid

He pulled the pearled seashell from his pack,
but then, with a start, he heard
the woman's voice calling him again: "Help me. Please don't be deterred."
The emotions he felt all came up again. Within him again they stirred.
She then told him the following tale, which he remembered word for word.

"What the old man said is truly the path, so please continue on,
for the Druid does indeed exist and is someone you can depend upon.
I know it for a fact, you know, as I was once one of his two wives."
As she spoke, she wept and said,
"It's in your hands whether my life survives.

"You'll find him in the deep dark forest on a narrow path
just north then west.
He'll be the one standing there with a staff,
and on his tunic a cross for a crest,
for he is the revered and holy Arch Druid,
the oldest and the one most wise.
He'll be dressed in a cloak and robes of gold,
but don't look directly into his eyes.

"You'll know you're close when you pass
a boundary formed by a boxwood hedge
that surrounds a small open clearing with sacred oak trees at its edge."
And then, just like that, her voice disappeared,
but he knew what he must do.
He got his bearings in his mind
and started walking north and then west, too.
Following the narrow forest path as it weaved,
he was determined to follow through.
And sure enough, he came to a hedge.
As he squeezed past, the clearing came into view.

There in the middle stood a tall man
surrounded by fey creatures and loyal beasts.
All around stood massive trees of old sacred oaks
like petrified wooden priests.
At the sides of the Arch Druid were other Druids
in different hooded cloaks—
some white but other colors, too, all tied at their waists with ropes.

The Arch Druid turned to address the young man and said,
"I don't interact with civilized folk."
The young man pulled out the pearled seashell and replied,
"From this shell your wife spoke."
He relayed the story that she had told,
then waited for the Arch Druid's response.
The elder rubbed his long white beard with his hand,
then said, "I think I know what she wants."

Tales of a Witch

"I don't mean my wife when I say that, no,
it's definitely someone else, indeed.
It's got to be the Witch, I think,
who wants to draw me in and mislead.
She's been after my Druid blood for years.
Yes, that much is guaranteed.
So she's taken my wife as bait, I presume, in order to succeed.

"That's not all the Witch has done,
for wives and daughters have disappeared.
With the story you have told me, young man,
it is what I have most feared,
that she is kidnapping women and girls for experiments for her tests,
trying different potions and spells on them, for this is what it suggests."

The Arch Druid called out to the others,
"Don your cloaks of grey bull hides,
for the time has come to battle the Witch,
and our fey ones will be our guides."

To the young man, he said, "We must beware of the Hounds,
for they protect and guard the Witch by patrolling around her grounds.
They are the three-headed Ghostly Hounds, the ones at her command.
When we hear their snarls and growls, we'll know we're close at hand.

"Then we'll have to find the Witch's lair,
for they say it's hidden underground.
If we're able to do all that, young man,
my wife and the others will be found.

"But we'll still have to deal with the wicked Witch,
and that won't be an easy task.
And to ensure that the Witch can't identify me,
each one of us will wear a mask.

"Take this magic nightshade sword, young man, and if you have a chance,
slash the Witch with its sharp, poisoned blade
before she puts you into a trance."
Then moving stealthily through the woods as the night bid the day farewell,
off they went in search of the Witch and the one calling from the shell.

The Battle with the Ghostly Hounds

The moon was full and cast its light, its reflections on weapon blades
of swords and axes carried on their backs
as they walked through the forest glades.
But then these words from the seashell spoke
in a voice sounding so sincere,
"Tread carefully now, all ye brave men,
for you'll find the Hounds quite near."

With his hand cupped to his ear, the Arch Druid
heard howls coming from the Hounds.
And in that moment, everyone froze and listened to the sounds.

The Druids drew out their weapons, and as the tension grew,
the Arch Druid said, "Stand fast, men. Your courage will see us through."
And as they moved silently forward so carefully and quietly,
they all knew what lay ahead for them, and caution was the key.

All at once, the dogs were upon them, and chaos then ensued
as Hounds' jaws snapped and crunched the bones
of Druids the dogs pursued.
They came from all directions, their shapes translucent and unearthly.
The young man and Druids fought bravely, but what was their fate to be.

There were cries for help and screams as well coming from the dark.
Both men and dogs were falling fast from blows that made their mark.
The Hounds' fangs dripped Druid blood, but there were yelps as well.
The Druids and young man gathered their strength
with forceful efforts to quell

the Ghostly Hounds, protectors of the Witch, and fighting took its toll.
But the Druids with their swords and axes began to take control.
And then finally it all ended. Only panting and moans were heard.
The last of the Hounds lay dead on the ground. Not another thing stirred.

The men breathed hard and fast, then addressed any injury
while the Arch Druid reminded all those left of their responsibility
to find the opening to the Witch's lair, for it was underground.
He ordered the men to take their staffs and use them to pound

the area they were standing in, to check it all around.
Nothing else was then heard except thumping of staffs on the ground
till one staff finally hit its mark with a thump, thump, and clink.
The young man looked on and thought, *Is this the missing link?*

Into the Witch's Lair

They cleared away the forest debris to find a circular metal cover.
They pulled it off, and with surprise, here is what they would discover:
a large shaft that went down underground with a ladder on its side wall.
The Arch Druid pulled the young man aside and said,
"Here's what I propose, but it's your call.

"I think you should go down alone for now to rescue the ones below.
We can bring them up to safety here and guard, but I worry, even so.
If you encounter the Witch, do not engage, for she will overpower you.
Yell out and call us to your aid, and a deathly deed we will do."

The young man entered the shaft alone with a mask covering his face.
His nightshade sword strapped on his back, he descended into dark space.
When he finally reached the floor below with his eyes trying to adjust,
he thought of the journey that had led him there
and whose voice had placed her trust.

For that was what it was all about, to save the woman who had called
through the magic of a pearled seashell,
which had held his mind enthralled.
As he made his way down the passageway,
he saw openings barred with steel
and women and girls with their faces to the bars to plead and to appeal.

"Please save us, young man," they cried out, their hands gripping the bars.
He knelt and with his dagger pried while they prayed aloud to the stars.
He eventually jerked a lock with his knife, and they all heard the click.
as the metal gate opened at last, he told them, "You must be quick."

"Go and climb the ladder at the end, for the Druids are waiting for you.
They will protect, and you will be safe, for they are tried and true."
He continued doing the same to each holding cell he passed,
each woman and girl then no longer a Witch's pawn and truly free at last.

The Woman in the Mourning Cloak
But he hadn't seen one who wore a mourning cloak,
so he asked where she might be.
They told him through the last door on the left
in a bamboo cage he would see
the one that he was looking and searching for. He ran down to the door
and pushed it open, and before him was the one whose fate he had sworn

to free, the woman who had spoken to him
through the beautiful pearled seashell.
The woman said, "I knew you'd come to free me from this Witch's cell."
He cut the bamboo into shreds and extended his hand to help her out.
She said, "But first I must see your face, young man,
so I have no further doubt."

She reached up with her hands and removed his mask and exclaimed,
"It's you!"
And with tears streaming down her face, she cried, "I knew . . . I knew . . .
I knew.
Do you know who you are?" she asked, hugging him closely to her then,
for I have a story about a miracle, which brought us together again.

"You see, I wear this mourning cloak for a special one in my heart,
for I once had a child, a teenaged boy, and since we've been apart,
I wear this cloak in remembrance of him, thinking he was no more,
and trapped in this cage I summoned the gods,

and this is what I asked for:

"to see his face again someday, and this is what they said to me:
'Someone will find a pearled seashell by the shore. We promise this will be.
And when you talk, he will hear your voice and listen to your plea.
That someone will truly be your son, and he'll return to you. You'll see.'

"You're my son, the one I lost!" she said. The gods had made it true
all because of a pearled seashell found on the shore near a sea of blue.
But if you, dear reader, think that this is it, the happy ending of our tale,
it won't be the case because of what lies ahead behind a mirrored veil.

He took his mother by the arm, and they ran together to the end.
He glanced back and saw a shadow moving just around the other bend.
Have I forgotten anyone else? was the thought he had.
His mother pleaded with him to come. She anticipated something bad.

The End Game in The Room of Mirrors
His mother cried out from the ladder,
"Please wait for the Druids to help you!"
But he was already running back and rounded the bend and out of view.
He saw a door ahead that reflected his image but recognized it as just a veil.
Observing closer, he found it a mirrored cloth, and then he heard this wail,

"What you've done to me, young man, you're going to regret."
He pushed aside the veil and drew his sword. His body in a cold sweat,
he entered slowly into a room, and in every direction he faced
saw only his own reflection there, a room full of mirrors. As his heart raced,
he couldn't tell what was back or front or what was left or right.
Was there a step ahead or to the side, or was it a trick upon his sight?
He took a step and bumped into mirrors but managed to step around some

not knowing if he'd been there before or where he'd just come from.
Then an eerie, echoing, cackling laugh erupted in a high pitch,
and a voice said,
"Welcome, young man. You have a date with the Witch."
He started to bash the mirror panes with the handle of his sword,
and as they broke and shattered on the floor, he made his way forward.

He stopped himself just short, thank God, from a hole gaping in the floor.
He caught his balance at the last second.
One more step, and he'd have been no more.
He knew that's what the Witch was hoping, that he'd step and he'd be gone.
Down that hole that showed no bottom,
he'd keep falling on and on and on.

He turned around to see only three mirrored panes that remained.
The image of the Witch was in all three, leaving it all unexplained.
He looked carefully at each mirror, wondering which one was the true.
He would have to decide quickly—that he was sure he knew.

Just then he felt faint and dizzy. Was she putting a spell on him?
He tried to lift up his sword arm, but heaviness weighed his limb.
He slowly sank down to his knees, and things looked very grim,
and he realized in that moment, he was surely at her whim.

With a grin on her face, the Witch stepped forward
from the middle mirror,
cautiously approaching till close to him. As she moved nearer,
he reached up and grabbed her sleeve,
pulling her toward him with all his might.
The two of them entwined as one,
falling into the hole and then out of sight.

Just as the Druids entered the room to witness the frightful scene,
—the young man and the wicked Witch, in the room where they had been
and the next moment gone from sight—seeing them both disappear.
The only sounds heard were screams from the Witch,
who fell in complete fear.

They raced over to the bottomless pit, knelt, and looked down to scan,
but they knew in their hearts it was the
end of the Witch and the end of the young man.

The Final Resting Place
The waters under the Witch caves, the watery path, had led,
carrying him along with currents to a place by the river bed.
The tales say where his body was found, and this they also said:
nothing was found of the Witch but her hat,
so they knew she was also dead.

The Druids laid him gently down in a serene spot under oak trees,
and all were there to honor him on a day with a light breeze.
They'd always remember his memory and also his life that he gave.
They all knelt in silence as they lowered him into his grave.

The women and girls gathered there, the ones whom he had saved,
and in their hearts, they silently wept, and him they all praised.
Each and every one gave thanks for a special young man, indeed,
who had heeded the call and rescued them in their hour of need.

Surrounding them were the Druids, fey creatures, and loyal beasts,
and the one who loved him most of all, lastly but certainly not least,
his mother who laid some daisies down, then blew a kiss farewell.
She placed on his grave a remembrance for him,
a carved stone pearled seashell.

Abalene

Abalene, Abalene, a child so wee,
born to wife, Rebecca, and husband, Lee,
her a candlemaker with varied scents so fine,
him a laborer in vineyards for a distiller of wine,

Abalene, Abalene, a small baby girl,
to them a true treasure like a pure pearl.
But poor Lee and Rebecca cried out loud,
for their infant child they had had to enshroud

due to the announcement of the royal decree.
The edict stated any girl born in the land must be
brought to the castle. They were thus commanded,
and any who defied would be marked and branded,

for it was told by the royal seers on high
that a female born of that year was drawing nigh.
She eventually would usurp the royals who ruled,
but the town folk knew better and could not be fooled,

because they had heard that girls brought there
were not seen again nor seen anywhere.
The rumor was the seers did the deadly misdeed,
all infant females to be removed for them to succeed.

With resignation, Lee and Rebecca made up their minds.
Talking secretly together after closing the blinds,
they decided they would hide Abalene to protect her life,
that most difficult decision made by husband and wife.

So to the one whose life was dedicated to others they went,
to the only one considered trustworthy, to ask his assent.
They brought Abalene to the shelter of Melodious, the monk,
the babe hidden and covered up in a wicker trunk.

They then unveiled her to the ascetic for his safekeeping.
Rebecca and Lee left her there, both of them weeping,
wondering if they'd ever see their little Abalene again,
but both resigned to that possibility, realized then.

Riding the roads only at night to be discreet,
the monk traveled by donkey to a mountain monastery retreat.
The babe hidden in the trunk, together they rode.
Ahead the terrain was getting steeper—it showed.

Melodious got off his donkey and, with the trunk in tow,
followed a remote path that only he knew where to go.
Holding the reins and trunk, on he strode,
till in his sight at last he saw the secluded, holy abode.

All those within the monastery made a solemn vow
to keep Abalene's presence there a secret somehow.
Melodious would watch over her safety, that he would see,
to fulfill his ultimate promise to Rebecca and Lee.

So, in the monastery did she grow and thrive.
As early years to run and play arrived,
Abalene explored all the sights within bounds
of the secluded monastery gardens and monastery grounds.

She didn't ask how she came to be there.
After all, it was all she knew—nothing of elsewhere.
Always happy and content in the company of the monk,
she and he sat talking quietly by his bunk

discussing nature's wonders, plants, herbs, and the universe
or outside under shade trees they would converse.
The history of everything inspired her with wonder,
or sometimes faery tales made her laugh or ponder.

Melodious doted on her every wish and need
and, as she grew, brought her books. He taught her to write and read,
and all there was to learn about numbers. He taught her math
so Abalene would be learned, for that was the path.

As she grew older with the knowledge she had gleaned,
it was time for the monk to show her a marvel thus far unseen,
for Melodious knew the destiny that awaited Abalene,
and she was a grown woman at age eighteen.

She followed him as he brought her up the mountainside
till they came to the opening of a cave high and wide.
They entered together into the dark
as Melodious made to her a surprising remark:

"Abalene, you are a woman with a destiny,
so hear me now and listen carefully."
He told the story of Rebecca and Lee.
Her parents he told her about, and she would see

why and how she came to be at the monastery near.
He then confided, "I may be a monk, but I'm also a seer,
and I know there is much in the future for you ahead.
We'll discuss it further, but for now, our purpose is here!" he said.

They continued to walk deeper in with torches held for lights.
Dripping drops of water from the ceiling hung stalactites,
Abalene sensed the air becoming warmer and dense,
and if not for Melodious at her side, she would have been tense.

They came into a large chamber, and what a sight to behold.
There lay a creature, its scales of white gold
with large wings wrapping its body enclosed
and long claws attached to each of its toes.

At their approach, its neck extended as it lifted its head.
With each breath from its nostrils did smoke spread.
It opened its eyelids to show its eyes large and red.
Its mouth revealed rows of sharp teeth ready to shred.

It swished its long tail around on the floor,
and suddenly it said, "I am the one you are looking for.
I am Braveheart, the dragon, for you Abalene."
Abalene was awestruck, so incredible the scene.

"Abalene, Abalene, I've been waiting for you so long.
Now that we've found each other, we can right the wrong,
for I am yours and yours alone.
The foretelling of the future through prophecy has been shown."

In the days that followed, Abalene went up to the cave
and listened to Braveheart for advice he gave,
especially how to stay on him when they would fly.
She trusted the dragon, and on him she would rely.

So she climbed onto his back by climbing his scales.
She marveled with respect at his golden details.
The legendary creature was hers alone.
His loyalty Braveheart had sworn and shown.

She grabbed onto his body as he began to take flight.
Abalene and her dragon were quite the sight.
His wings extended, out they flew up into the sky,
and she could see so much from being so high.

She loved the feeling of flying and feeling the breeze
as Braveheart glided and swooped low over the trees,
then soared quickly up again with her face in the headwind
and landed back at the cave when the days light dimmed.

So Abalene visited Braveheart every day,
and made plans for the time when they would fly away.
She then went to Melodious with her questions to ask:
"What is my destiny? What is my task?"

He said, "I always knew that this day would come.
Sit beside me, and I'll tell the tale of the land you're from.
The present ruler is evil with no moral code shown.
He inflicts cruelty and oppression from his throne.

"His armies defeated the good King Damir,
ever loved by all for so many years here.
The name Damir means to give peace to the world,
but the people are crushed and their heartache unfurled.

"Since his defeat, years have passed in this land of suffering and misery.
All those here and in exile expectantly await delivery.
As prophesies and visions have always foretold,
they say the savior is one with a dragon controlled."

Melodious then said, "I am not Melodious nor neither a monk,
but I knew you as the savior when I saw you in the wicker trunk.
I am truly King Damir with my vow to avenge all the ruler's wrongs.
So, our fate rests with your decision. To you only it belongs.

"I'll tell you also that this monastery is not what it seems,
for those who reside here also have dreams.
They are angels and archangels awaiting the reckoning,
the liberator, the salvation they have been beckoning.

"So now you know why I raised and protected you.
We pray that you and Braveheart will follow through
to remove the evils from this land.
To help, all good people will be at your command."

"Good King Damir," Abalene said, kissing his hand,
"with Braveheart, I'm with you. Together we stand.
We will rid this land of evil and cursed rule,
of the one who presides with rule so cruel."

King Damir sent out messengers throughout the lands
to prepare all good citizens for the savior's commands.
King Damir assembled holy armies of might,
for he envisioned a crusade for all good knights to fight.

Abalene sought out Braveheart for solace,
for she knew the devised plan would need to be flawless.
Thinking of her real parents so long apart,
she ran to the cave and curled up to Braveheart's dear heart,

but she wasn't afraid because she wasn't alone.
Her dragon beside her his loyalty had shown
that together they had a chance to defeat and dethrone,
to give back to the people the life they had previously known.

Armies gathered and marched, King Damir in the lead,
their banners flying and each armored knight on his steed.
Approaching close to the castle, they all did heed,
for ahead the evil king's soldiers waited, unwilling to concede.

King Damir knew his forces smaller and outmanned,
but then, he raised a finger on his right hand
to point up at the sky. Soldiers raised their eyes.
It astonished them to see a dragon circling in the skies.

For out of the misty fog flew a dragon so large.
It breathed fire from its mouth to release and discharge
and amazed all on the ground to see a woman riding its back.
She maneuvered the beast for its expected attack.

It scared soldiers in the castle out of their wits.
They ran as dragon fire continued with hits
to the castle walls and towers erupting in flame
as the dragon kept blasting with perfect aim.

They threw down their weapons and began to flee
as King Damir's armies marveled at what they did see,
but the evil king escaped by horseback. He galloped away
and looked afraid over his shoulder. He knew himself the next prey.

He neared forest edge, that bad king so cruel.
Abalene guided her dragon with skill and demeanor quite cool.
On the evil one, Braveheart descended while extending its talons
and plucked that king off the back of his black stallion.

The dragon carried him by robes clutched in its claws
for many miles—to his final destination it was.
The dragon released him in the middle of the sea,
dropped him into water out of sight, his destiny to be.

As for all the rest in this story of fate,
for years bards would sing tales of Abalene the Great
and, of course, King Damir and Braveheart, the dragon, too,
their destinies bound together all the way through.

King Damir ruled honorably in the years thereafter.
The people thrived and were so much happier,
but, of course, you want to know what happened to those special two,
Abalene and her winged dragon, with a please and thank you.

They had one last quest in order to find
Abalene's parents, whom she had left behind.
So they flew in search of the one called the candlemaker
and the one they knew only as the vineyard caretaker.

The story is told that her parents she found
with Braveheart gliding slowly till its feet touched the ground.
She jumped off his back as her parents looked shocked
to first see a dragon and then the young woman who walked

toward them, her face looking familiar in an unthinkable way.
Could it possibly be? Their minds quickly recalled that day
so long ago when a trusted monk took her away.
Could it be? Could it be Abalene?

"I'm Abalene, I'm Abalene," she cried, running toward them.
Then with hugs and joyous tears from all of them,
she said, "For eighteen long years, I have been away,
but I'm home now, and this is where I will stay.

"To be with you—that's how I wanted it to be,"
at long last back with her parents, Rebecca and Lee.
But one last thing had to be done.
Abalene turned to the dragon, her own special one.

"I will never forget you," she said, her arms 'round his neck.
And Braveheart replied, "Nor I you."

She watched him fly off and into the sunset,
that dragon of hers, in the distance a speck.

The One Who Couldn't See But Could

When she was in her room all alone in the dark,
she felt with her hands for a distinct mark,
that of a door knob that only she knew
to turn and open, to enter and pass through—

through a door in her room not really there,
through the portal she went totally aware.
For there she could see, her sight not impaired,
in a magic land her eyes repaired.

For in her real life, they consider her blind,
but in Faery Land, she could leave it behind.
She saw all the faery lights twinkling ahead,
and she wanted to follow to see where they led.

Up and around and in and out,
the faery lights shine all about
under and over their trails to light
the path of the faeries, oh, so bright.

Signs of their passage through the woods
shone through the darkness from where she stood,
and marveling at the lovely visual display
was the small girl who had slipped away.

She followed the lights and skipped along
while whistling the tune of her favorite song.
"Sometimes I say I cannot truly see,
but there are other times I can truly be free

"to see everything around in my sight,
true colors and images of every delight
revealing all to me through the thingamabob
which I do by twisting and turning a doorknob."

So there she was ready for new adventure,
for her motto was "nothing gained if nothing ventured."
Faeries led her till reaching the end of the woods,
then dropped a present, some candy goods.

She entered into pastures of purple and white phlox
and yellow sunflowers swaying on sturdy stalks,
the wheatfields in movement by touch of a breeze
as she listened to distinct buzzing sounds of bumblebees.

Green and red spotted hummingbirds buzzed alongside,
and her eyes could see every detail as if magnified.
They hovered in air with little wings beating fast,
the next second zooming off like a rocket blast.

Field mice scurried about searching for seeds of wheat.
Squirrels darted this way and that, their cheeks stuffed with treats.
Butterflies floated in rhythm in fluttering flight.
All those things and more she saw in the sunlight.

At a place under a tree called the Golden Hop,
she saw two rabbits arguing, so she crouched to eavesdrop.
One said, "I have no idea why you want to open a tobacco shop,"
while pulling the cork off a bottle they shared. Off it came with a pop.

"You know it's supposed to be bad for your teeth is what they say.
What would you do if your two front teeth fell out?"
he asked with dismay.
"There would be no more carrots for you to chew on,
buddy boy, but hey—
there's always crushed carrot mush to slurp through
a straw for your entrée."

An opossum hanging upside down from a tree limb above them called out,
"Quit your squabbling. Is this all you do during the whole day throughout?
When will you give me some quiet serenity and peace?"
The rabbits replied, "As soon as the blind girl who sees comes
with a candy piece."

The girl recognized the rabbits she had seen before and knew
the names of both the fluffy ones—Bob and Boo—
who, drinking and arguing, waited for her all day through
till she appeared with faery candy to give them to chew.

She stood up and waved and said, "Here I am!"
"Good," the opossum said. "Now you rabbits can
get your candy and scram."
Bob and Boo hopped over to get their treat.
Hugging her lower legs is how they would greet.

"We've been waiting so long, it's time for siesta,
but once our nap is done, we'll have a fiesta.
"Woohoo," they exclaimed as they hopped away.
"See you next time, little blind girl who sees," they did always say.

The opossum motioned her over with a wave of his feet,
then said, "The sun is so bright for you with all this heat,
so take my straw hat to give you some shade—"
The one tied with a string under his chin, the hat he had made.

He said, "I know your head is bigger than mine,
but if you give it a tug, it will automatically align."
He placed it on her head, and after a tug, it fit!
"Thank you, so much, Mr. Opossum, and I'd love to chat with you a bit,

"but I'm in somewhat of a hurry today, so I must go now lickety-split,
but when I'm done with my adventure, I'll come back to return it."
At the time, she noticed a palomino pony grazing nearby.
On its back, she saw a small package, bow, and ribbon tie.

The pony gently whinnied, and she knew it was heartfelt,
his way of saying hello. Bowing his head, on one leg he knelt
so she could reach up and untie the package he held on his back.
She held in her hands a small ebony box, its wood a perfect pitch black.

When she opened the lid, it played a soft music track—
when she opened the lid even a tiny crack.
In return, she offered him as a token of payback,
a treat from her pocket, a mint candy snack.

She asked, "Wherever did you find this marvelous music box?"
The pony replied. "When I was grazing, I found it nearby in the phlox.
I waited for you to come so I could present you with this gift—
for the blind girl that sees when she's in our midst."

"Thank you, Pony," she said and put it in her sack.
"I'll see you again the next time I come back."
She threw her pack over her shoulders and continued to walk
down to the river where she heard some strange talk.

"Oooohhh, sudsy, sudsy, scrub-a-dub clean,
covered with lather for our brush to glean
the dirt off till we're soft as silk with a fine sheen—
this is my daily pleasure and daily routine."

Holding a long-handled brush in two little hands floated the otter,
serene on his back in the midst of the water,
scrubbing his body while singing his song,
"Blind girl who sees, I've waited for you all day long."

"Hi, Otto," said the girl, as that's how he was called,
lying then on the bank, there drying all sprawled.
"I've prepared hors d'oeuvres for our lunch," Otto said
while placing the goodies on the blanket he spread.

The girl exclaimed, "What a nice meal to have by the riverbed."
"Yes," said the otter. "We have raspberries and salmon with French bread,
and for drinks, tonic water and ginger. Dig in. Go ahead!"
So they sat talking, catching up on their news—leaving nothing unsaid.

She enjoyed her time with Otto the otter, could tell him anything—
her favorite playmate friend in the world—he was the real thing.
She loved to hold him and feel his soft coat as he nuzzled,
and every time after their meal, that was how they snuggled.

She sat back on the grass as the day soon would be gone.
She watched Otto splish, splash, urging her to "Come on."
Sometimes she joined Otto in cool river water
where they played together, just her and the otter.

The sun went on down, and eventually all would be dark.
"Otto, I'm sorry, but time's here for me to go," she remarked,
for she knew before long it would be just like her room at home—
the real world with nothing but darkness till she let her mind roam.

She twisted the doorknob in her mind and returned to her world.
She wrapped herself in her blankets as her thoughts whirled.
Her adventure had ended for the time, but she had been free,
and she thought of the next one and what she would see.

She sat listening to tunes emanating from her music box,
the one the palomino pony had found in the phlox.
All her friends waited patiently for her to visit again:
Bob and Boo, Mr. Opossum, Pony, and Otto in their domain—

the faeries to lead her on the path back to them, and then,
they would have more adventures together over and over again.
Blind with no vision in the real world—that part is true,
but full of awareness wherever, she also well knew.

All she had to do, really, was reach out and touch,

the gateway to that world where she saw and enjoyed so much,

for in her mind and heart, she believed and knew,

even when you're blind, in your imagination, dreams can come true.

Camille's Legacy

In late nineteenth-century Paris, France, center of a vibrant new style of life, attracted people from all over the world. They came to admire the latest trends in fashion, art, and theater in a time of clear social class distinction between the haves and the have nots. Summer had finally arrived on an unusually warm morning as she hurried along the street. The woman carried a bag of cleaning supplies in one arm while clutching a child's hand in the other. The main boulevard bustled with people on their way to work, and shops they passed prepared to open for business. She and the child walked down one of the wide side streets lined with imposing stately homes. They stopped in front of one to the left on the street side enclosed by a wrought-iron fence. It had a large wraparound porch surrounded by beautiful trees and a wonderful privacy garden sheltered by flowering bushes. They climbed the front steps, and she knocked on the door. A plain looking woman of humble manner and lowly means, she arrived each day to clean and do housekeeping chores for Madame Didier, owner of the residence.

"Bonjour, Mme. Gauthier. I see you have a little helper today," Mme. Didier's butler, Odilon, said as he opened the door.

That day, Mme. Gauthier brought along Lily, her twelve-year-old daughter. Mme. Gauthier hoped perhaps to find additional work for Lily in order to help supplement her own meager wages. When asked, Mme. Didier raised her eyebrows and said she thought the request impertinent but perhaps the girl could do some sweeping or fold linen to keep busy. As Mme. Didier passed the butler, she whispered "Keep an eye on the little one. Could have sticky fingers, you know."

Mme. Didier wouldn't tolerate a thief in her house.

Mme. Gauthier and Lily didn't have much. They lived in a dark and dreary one-room flat, the entry located down an alleyway full of stray cats and just off the main boulevard. They had only one appliance, a stove for cooking or heat. Lily never knew her father, and her mother never spoke of him. For as long as she could remember, her mother had worked as a cleaning lady. They got by, but just barely.

On the other hand, the Didier family was quite well off. A retired officer in the French Foreign Legion, M. Didier had done quite well for himself moving up through the ranks. After he retired, he built a successful business in trade and became a wealthy entrepreneur. They lived in their grand home surrounded by others in one of the Paris arrondissements.

Lily stood in the front foyer of the Didier home. A mansion, she thought as she looked around. She saw large paintings in elaborate gold frames hanging from the walls, tall Chinese porcelain vases arranged just so, half round cast iron fireplaces with massive carved oak surrounds supporting mantel shelves above each with ornate clocks, sculptured busts placed on marble stands, a wide dark mahogany wood staircase leading from the foyer to the next level, ornate wallpaper of flower designs covering the walls, and oriental runners on the floors. She had never seen anything like it in all her life.

Her mother told her not to dilly-dally, as she had a job to do. Handing Lily a broom, her mother said, "One of your jobs each day is to sweep the wraparound porch."

Lily went outside to do her work. As she did, she noticed a girl about her age in a beautiful pale-yellow dress walking toward the house from the gardens.

"I'm Camille. Who are you?"

"I'm Lily," said Lily quietly, her head bowed slightly, as she wasn't sure she should talk with anyone when she was supposed to be working.

"Lily, what a lovely name! Lilies are my favorite flowers," said Camille excitedly. "Meet me in the gardens before you go home today, say in three hours?" she continued as she looked at her watch enclosed in a bracelet of fine gold and blue sapphires.

Lily returned inside and continued chores, folding linens, dusting, and whatever else her mother asked of her. Lily kept looking at the clocks as she worked. When three hours had passed, she went out of the house and along the pathway to the gardens beyond. It felt peaceful and secluded as low-lying trees and flowering azaleas and rhododendrons blocked the view of the house except for the roof and chimneys peaking above.

Camille sat on a stone bench in front of a three-tiered water fountain, the only sound trickling water as it sprayed from the fountain spout into circular basins of rock. When she saw Lily, Camille jumped up, ran over to her, and gave Lily a hug. "I'm so glad you came," she said.

Surrounded by the pleasant aroma of lilacs, they sat side by side on the bench. "What a beautiful place this garden is," said Lily.

"My favorite place," replied Camille. "I don't get to have many friends."

"Why?" asked Lily.

Camille hesitated a moment, then explained, "I have a disease, and I don't know how much longer I will be here, so I come to the gardens to contemplate and ponder the meanings of life." Nevertheless, she smiled brightly and said, "That's why I'm so glad you're here."

Camille noticed a mark on Lily's neck and asked, "What's that mark on your neck?"

Lily reached up with her hand to touch it. "It's a birthmark in the shape of a lily. That's where I got my name."

Camille exclaimed, "I love lilies of all types. And we're going to be the best of friends."

"I'd like that, too," Lily said, "but I must get back to the house, as my mother will be leaving soon."

"Okay," said Camille, "but promise me you'll meet me here every day at three."

"I will," Lily said confidently.

They stood up, gave each other a hug, and walked hand in hand back up the path leading to the grand home.

Mme. Didier saw them approach and, with a scowl, went to Camille and grabbed her by the hand. As she tugged Camille to separate them, Lily heard her say, "What were you thinking, being with that girl?"

Camille asked, "Why?"

Her mother said, "Don't you know your station? You can't associate with that type. What would people say?"

"What would people say?" Camille asked.

"They'd say," Mme. Didier replied, "'Shame on someone of high status even talking with someone of the lower class.' It's just not done, I say," and she dragged Camille away.

Lily well knew her status in life—at the bottom. She and Camille lived worlds apart in terms of how society perceived a person's rank. She knew it, but she also knew deep inside herself that it was not right.

But what could she do? She knew in the future that she would live her life as her mother did, cleaning rich people's houses. Maybe it wasn't right, but it was just the way it was.

Nevertheless, the next day, as the clocks struck three, Lily sneaked out to follow the garden path to the water fountain. And there was Camille, grinning. Camille said, "I don't care what my mother said. I've been alone for so long, and anyway, I don't agree with any of those hurtful things she said. That's not who I am. I've sat on this bench every day thinking about my sickness and the meaning of the time I have left.

"What better purpose do I have than to help one who has less than I, say a best friend?" she asked with a smile. "When I know it's close to the time I must leave this world, I will place my watch of gold with blue sapphires under this rock here by the bench. It is my gift to you. If you are ever of need of something important—food, clothes, or a better place to live that you can't afford, you can sell it. It is worth a lot of money and will provide you some temporary comfort."

"I'd never sell it," said Lily. "I'd always keep it. I would treasure it because it's from my best friend." And she hugged Camille tightly. Always careful not to be seen, they had many more days in the gardens together. As best friends will do, they shared secrets and stories. With Camille cooped up in her house, Lily told her stories about the city, including about her favorite pastry shop on the cobbled street of Rue Denoyez or about when she went up to Montmartre to watch artists paint and sketch or times she strolled along the Left Bank to see booksellers' stalls or watch the flea circus.

Camille listened intently to Lily's tales and clapped her hands when each story finished. And so they spent their time, growing closer as best friends do.

But then came the day when Camille was not there.

Nor the next day. Or the next.

M. Didier climbed the steep steps from the sidewalk up one flight from street level. Reaching the top, he saw hazelnut and chestnut trees surrounding a small courtyard and, in the background, cages containing rabbits. To his right was the entrance to the clock repairer's place of business. The bell hanging above the door jingled as M. Didier entered the shop. Behind the counter sat a heavy set man. He leaned over and squinted through a scope as he busily worked on a small piece of jewelry with the tools in his hands. He wore the short magnifying lens on a strap around his bald head.

"Bonjour, M. Bertrand. Comment allez-vous?" The clockmaker looked up from his work.

"Ah, M. Didier, what can I do for you?"

M. Didier reached into a leather pouch attached to his belt and pulled out a little watch enclosed in a bracelet of fine gold. The intricate pattern of gold metal held blue sapphires in its beautiful design.

"I would like you to take a look at this jewelry piece. Lately I have had to replace this watch and sapphire bracelet many times because my daughter Camille keeps losing them. She tells me they somehow come off her wrist and doesn't know where they fell. It's becoming very expensive. I then have to go out and buy a new one, exactly the same. But she's my daughter, and she loves it, so what can I do? Perhaps the clasps aren't tight enough. I was hoping you might find why they keep falling off."

"Of course," replied M. Bertrand, taking the watch bracelet from M. Didier. "Come back next Thursday, and in the meantime, I'll try to find out what the issue is."

That night, when Lily and her mother arrived home, she told Lily to sit next to her because she had something important to tell her. "I was told today by Odilon that Camille has become very sick and is bed bound," she said. Apparently, her mother said, the Didier family prepared for the worst.

Not long after receiving the information from her mother, Lily stood near the street corner of her home and watched from the alleyway as a procession passed. Bells from the church nearby had pealed all morning. Two altar boys carrying a cross walked first down the road followed by a priest reading the Bible, then a white carriage pulled by one white horse and inside a smaller-than-average white casket.

White lilies covered the top of the carriage. Behind the carriage, carrying his hat, walked a man wearing the uniform of the French Foreign Legion. All in black with black veils over their heads that hung back and front to their waists, three women followed him, then some twenty men from the armed forces, and a few civilians.

In the street, people gathered, some with their bikes, to watch the procession.

Lily knew her friend was gone. She also recognized lilies as Camille's favorite flowers. Had a flower, a name, and birthmark bonded their short time together? Lily and lilies? She would never know.

Then she remembered the gold watch with sapphires, something tangible that she could hold in her hands, a remembrance from the heart of a best friend. She wanted to keep it always and think of Camille every time she looked at it, a small blessing.

She raced to the Didiers' home and sneaked into the garden through the wrought-iron fence bordering the garden. When she reached the water fountain, she knelt down and turned over their secret rock. The watch bracelet wasn't there but in its place, a folded note. She opened it and read, "Go to #55 Rue de la Croix, Bertrand's clock repair shop. Your gift from me awaits you there, but if asked you must say you are me." It was signed "Camille."

Lily put the note into her pocket and made her way to the clock shop. When she came to #55, she climbed steep steps to the courtyard and saw the small shop to her right. She walked in, marveling at all the clocks. All ticking and tocking in rhythm, mantle clocks, grandfather clocks, cuckoo clocks, and clocks on bases made of cherub figures greeted her.

M. Bertrand heard the bell jingle when Lily arrived. Concentrating on his work, he hunched over a desk.

Without looking up, he asked, "What can I do for you?"

Lily replied "I'm here to pick up my watch."

"Which watch?"

"The one with the gold bracelet and sapphires," she replied.

"Ah," M. Bertrand said, unaware of the funeral nor of Camille's illness. "You must be M. Didier's daughter. I wondered why he hadn't come back for it."

Putting his work down, he proceeded to unlock the case under the countertop and pulled out the bracelet. "Here you go," he said, placing it in her hand. "I couldn't find a reason why you might be losing them. The clasp is tight. No need to pay me now. Your father can settle his account the next time he comes in. Just sign for it here."

Lily took the pen and wrote "Camille Didier."

Time passed. Every night, Lily unwrapped the bejeweled watch bracelet to hold in her hands while she said a prayer to Camille in heaven.

One day after work, her mother said, "I'm going straight home to start dinner. Would you please stop by the baker's and pick up a baguette." Lily loved going into that shop on the cobbled street of Rue Denoyez and headed to the bakery. As she entered, her sense of smell perked up with smells of fresh bread, pastries, croissants, turnovers, cakes, and fancy desserts.

She took a few satisfying whiffs, picked out a baguette, and put her coins on the counter top. M. Alard, the elderly baker and proprietor, scooped up the coins, then looked at her as if he was contemplating something.

After a few seconds he said "You come in here often. What is your name?"

"Lily," Lily replied.

His brow furrowed thoughtfully.

"Lily," M. Alard repeated. "Hmmmm. A young lady came in here a few months ago dressed high class, if you know what I mean. She said her name was Camille. She asked me to hold onto a special item until her best friend, Lily, came by. She requested I pass on the item to her friend.

"She persisted, and I decided I would do what she asked.

"She did insist I make sure I gave the item to the right Lily. She said to ask to see the girl's birthmark in the shape of a lily, and I would know I had the right girl."

Lily turned down her collar to display the mark on her neck. "Then you're the one," M. Alard said as he reached to shelving behind the counter, picked something up, and handed Lily a small packet wrapped in blue felt and tied with string.

"It's yours," he said.

Lily didn't know what to make of it all.

Camille had been here? Why? How long ago did he say? And left something for her? She drew the string and opened the felt packet. In her hands was a watch enclosed in a bracelet of fine gold and blue sapphires. Exactly like her other one. She also noticed a tiny scroll tied with a ribbon. "Wow", said M. Alard as he leaned over the countertop. "That is a special item. Worth a lot of money, that one is. Nice to have such friends, I'd say."

Lily rewrapped the package, put it in her pocket, and walked out.

That night, Lily unwrapped the package with the watch and the tiny scroll. She loosened the tie and read the note. "To my best friend, Lily, my gift to you, to do the things you most want to do." It was signed Camille and had a stamped mark of a picture of a lily.

Time passed. Every night Lily unwrapped the two bejeweled watch bracelets to hold in her hands while she said a prayer to Camille in heaven.

When weekends arrived and Lily had the days off from work at the Didiers', she walked the streets of Montmartre as they wound their way up the hill. She loved to stand and watch artists pull out their easels, put on blank canvases, and then masterfully create beautiful scenes in wonderful colors of paint. Some would use pastel while others drew or sketched on thick paper sheets with pencil or charcoal sticks. She spent hours marveling at their talent.

One day, she noticed a sketch artist with a short-trimmed beard who wore a hand-knitted wool beret. He did quick portraits for Parisians passing by, and she thought his work quite good. He glanced at her as she looked over his shoulder at the portrait he worked on.

"Would you like your portrait done, Mademoiselle?"

Lily didn't say anything. He must know her status, she thought, and that she certainly couldn't afford even a few francs.

"No money?" he asked. "No matter. Sit down. I need the practice."

She didn't believe it. She thought him very talented, so why would he do it for free?

Nevertheless, she sat on the stool facing him. He looked at her intently, then began to sketch with pencil and ink, his eyes moving from her to his paper, back and forth. While he worked, he asked her, "Your name wouldn't happen to be Lily would it?"

"Yes, it is," she replied, surprised.

"Lily," the artist repeated. "Hmmmm. You know, what a coincidence. A young lady came to me here a few months ago, dressed smartly, and sat for her portrait. I found her exceptionally interesting. She told me her name was Camille, and she came from a very wealthy family. She made a very unusual request—to hold a special item until her best friend Lily came by. And if that was the case, she requested I pass on the item to her friend. But she did insist to make sure I would give the item to the right Lily. She said to ask to see the birthmark in the shape of a lily, and then I would know that that was the right girl."

Lily was shocked but her hand went to her collar and held it down, displaying the mark on her neck.

"Then you're the one," the artist said, reaching into a drawer on an easel next to him that he kept for displaying his work. He brought out a small packet wrapped in blue felt and tied with string. "This is yours, I guess," he said, handing it to her. "Your friend Camille paid me well to hold on to this, so here is your portrait, too, free of charge. Good luck, Lily. May your future be bright."

Clutching the packet in one hand and her portrait in the other, Lily hurried from the crowded main street. Ducking into a small alleyway for privacy, she stopped, breathing heavily.

What just happened? Lily wondered. Camille had sat for the artist? How long ago, did he say?

Lily drew the string and opened the felt. In her hands was a watch enclosed in a bracelet of fine gold and blue sapphires along with a tiny scroll tied with a blue ribbon. She loosened the tie and read the note, "To my best friend Lily, my gift to you, to do the things you most want to do." Camille had signed the note and stamped mark of a picture of a lily, exactly like her other two.

Time passed. Every night, Lily unwrapped the three bejeweled watch bracelets to hold in her hands while she said a prayer to Camille in heaven.

On a warm, sunny Saturday morning as Lily passed by the park she saw elderly Frenchmen engaged in one of their favorite pastimes, playing petanque. They threw a small wooden ball and then competed to see who could come closest to it when tossing their metal balls, called boules. Other men sat nearby at small tables engrossed in games of chess.

Lily loved the walk to one of her favorite places, the Left Bank. She crossed the bridge over the Seine River near Notre Dame Cathedral. Booksellers gathered in their stalls to show off their many wares—historical books, prints, and photographs. As Lily walked through the exciting environment, she watched the hustle and bustle of vendors hawking their inventory or arguing with potential customers about prices. Her purpose that morning focused on the spot she enjoyed most, the flea circus.

Ahead, Lily saw a small crowd gathered around the stall housing the attraction. Since there was no charge, she could stay as long as she wanted. At the end of the performance, someone would pass a hat to collect donations for the master of the acts.

She wiggled her way through bystanders to get a good vantage point up front. The way the fleas pulled miniature carts or other items enthralled her, and the master even had some holding tiny umbrellas and walking on thin wires attached over the table. She jumped with delight and clapped her hands after each act.

The man in charge, the circus master, sometimes took a puff from his pipe and grinned at the reactions of the spectators. As the hat passed at the end of the show, he caught Lily's eye and seemed a little bewildered.

"What's your name?" he asked.

"Lily," she replied.

He paused a second, then said, "Hmmmm. You may be the one I've been waiting for. A few months ago, a young lady politely asked me to do a favor for her. She was apparently from a well-to-do family here in Paris, I'd say, by the way she dressed and conducted herself—said her name was Camille."

Lily stood in shock.

"Yes," he continued. "Her request to me was to hold onto a special item until her best friend, Lily, came by. And if that happened, I should pass on the item to her friend. But she did insist to make sure I would be giving the item to the right Lily. She said to ask to see the birthmark in the shape of a lily. Then I would know that that was the right girl."

Lily slowly pulled her collar to the side to show the mark.

"Then you're the one," the circus master said, reaching over for a small box tucked among the many flea contraptions on his back table. He handed Lily a small packet wrapped in blue felt and tied with string. "It's yours," he said.

Well, we know the story by now, don't we?

Once away from the crowds, Lily drew the string and opened the felt. In her hands reposed a watch enclosed in a bracelet of fine gold and blue sapphires along with a tiny scroll tied with a blue ribbon. She loosened the tie and read the note. "To my best friend, Lily, my gift to you, to do the things you most want to do." Camille had signed it and stamped mark of a picture of a lily, exactly like her other three.

Time passed. Every night, Lily unwrapped the four bejeweled watch bracelets to hold in her hands while she said a prayer to Camille in heaven.

ⓒⓒ ⓓⓓ

Lily realized what Camille was trying to do for her, her best friend. Camille had visited each of the places in Paris Lily had told her about when they talked in the gardens. But how had she done it? That was a mystery to ponder. Had Odilon sneaked her out of the house so that, knowing Lily would return to those favorite places, she could leave her gifts?

Lily knew Camille had a watch in gold with sapphires, but where did she get three more, exactly the same? What Lily didn't know was the conversation between M. Didier and M. Bertrand at the clock repair shop many months prior and how M. Didier was baffled by the fact that Camille kept losing her bracelets.

She hadn't lost them at all. She had entrusted them to people who would pass them on to the true Lily, the one with a lily birthmark. Camille had left Lily a small fortune. Camille had given Lily the opportunity for a more prosperous life. But as her promise to Camille, Lily never sold the bracelets.

A few years later as Lily was about to enter M. Alard's bakery on the cobbled street of Rue Denoyez when she noticed a sign in his storefront window, "For Sale."

"Bonjour, Lily. What can I do for you?" M. Alard asked as she approached the counter.

"Are you really selling your bakery?" Lily asked.

"Well," he replied, "I'm not getting any younger, and Mme. Alard says it's getting to be too much for me, up at the crack of dawn to begin baking every morning and then being on my feet all day. I wouldn't mind being here part time, but it appears likely there'll be new owners here eventually."

Lily paid for her baguette and left.

She had an idea. She made her way to the nearest bank and asked to speak to someone about a loan. She was directed to a seat in front of a desk of one of the clerks.

"What can I do for you?" he asked, not looking up from his paperwork.

"I would like a loan," Lily replied. He raised his eyes from his work to see a bedraggled young woman sitting across from him. He looked at her as though she were a starving stray cat in the alleyway.

"Don't waste my time," he said.

Lily pulled out the pouch tied to her belt and methodically placed four watch bracelets of gold and sapphires on the table top. The clerk almost fell off his chair in surprise. He backed away and rose from his seat. "Let me get the manager," he said.

The manager scurried out of his office, the clerk right behind. He looked at Lily, then the gold bracelets, and motioned to the bank agent de sécurité.

"How do I know you didn't steal these?" he asked.

"My friend Camille gave them to me," Lily answered.

"Camille who?" asked the manager.

"Camille Didier."

"And how did she get them?"

"I don't know."

The manager knew M. Didier and addressed Lily. "Stay put!"

He instructed a courier to fetch M. Didier.

When M. Didier arrived, the manager took him aside and explained the situation. M. Didier had never seen Lily before. But when he went to pay for the watch at M. Bertrand's place of business, M. Bertrand told him his daughter had already picked it up. Camille had died, so he couldn't understand what young girl took it. It all became clear.

The bank manager and M. Didier approached Lily.

"How did you meet my daughter?" M. Didier asked. Lily told him how her mother and she provided cleaning services for Mme. Didier. She explained she had met Camille one day while sweeping the porch and Camille had asked her to spend time together in the gardens. Every day Lily's mother worked there with Lily, the two grew closer and became best friends.

"How do I know this to be true?" he asked.

Lily reached into her pocket and said, "Camille left me these personal scrolls."

M. Didier read the original note left long ago under the rock, then unrolled each scroll. He gazed down at them silently. He recognized Camille's handwriting and her favorite stamp mark, the lily. It tugged at his heart, because he had given that stamp to his daughter on her tenth birthday.

As a tear trickled down M. Didier's face, he looked at Lily and smiled, then turned to the bank manager and said, "Well, it appears everything here is in order."

Then he turned to Lily and said, "You're a special girl if my daughter Camille regarded you as her best friend." Then he turned again to leave the building.

As he walked away, Lily cried out, "No, sir. It was Camille. She was the special one."

The manager sat again across from Lily.

"Now what is it we can do for you?" he asked.

Lily offered the following proposal. The bank would provide the amount of the loan she requested. In return, she would leave three bracelets in safekeeping by the bank as collateral. Should she not meet the requirements of loan payments the bank would keep the number of bracelets whose value on the market equalled the value of the outstanding loan.

After all, Lily had made a commitment to Camille when she told Camille she would never sell the bracelets even though Camille had said she could. Born into the upper class, Camille figured she knew how society worked. The fact that priceless bracelets were in Lily's possession gave Lily significant negotiating power.

The bank manager agreed to the terms. They signed documents, and Lily left with her loan and the original bracelet gifted by Camille.

When Lily returned home, she asked her mother to sit with her. Clasping her mother's hands, she explained in detail everything that had happened—becoming best friends with Camille long ago, the bracelets Camille had left as gifts, Lily's experience at the bank, and her plans for the two of them to buy the bakery. They could afford to rent a much better apartment.

Her mother looked at Lily in wonder and amazement—surprised, thankful, and proud of her daughter.

They talked long into the night. They could begin a new life, a much better life.

The next morning, carrying their suitcases, they left their one-room flat off the alley.

As they entered the bakery on the cobbled street of Rue Denoyez, M. Alard looked up and greeted them. "Bonjour, Mme. Gauthier. Bonjour, Lily."

He wasn't sure why they had suitcases in hand, but Lily motioned him aside and offered him her proposal. She would buy the bakery outright, and she and her mother move into the empty flat just above the store. In addition, Lily proposed that M. Alard remain, at least part time, to teach her mother baking skills she would need to keep the business operating as it had done in the past.

M. Alard was very pleased with the proposed arrangement, since he could keep a hand in the business while only working when inclined. The arrangement fit his needs.

Lily and M. Alard signed the papers and shared a bottle of wine to consummate the deal.

M. Alard and Mme. Gauthier got along just fine, and she learned quickly. Her canelés de Bordeaux made with French rum and vanilla cake made a local hit along with her macaroons with raspberry filling and pistachios. Together, M. Alard and Mme. Gauthier increased the variety of their pastries, eclairs, pies, breads, and cakes. Everyone in the city soon raved about the new owners and Gauthier's Bakery recognized for fine service and quality. Lily waited on customers and, with M. Alard's guidance, attended to related financial matters. The business flourished.

Their new flat was much more spacious, and they loved living in the Paris neighborhood called Belleville with its sidewalk cafés and street art. Lily bought new clothes for her and her mother, and they decorated their flat to make it into a homey and pleasing environment for them to live. She paid the bank loan as agreed, and their lives were so much better. Lily was a realist and while not forgetting her past, was grateful for the miracle passed to her from Camille, her best friend.

Time passed. Every night Lily unwrapped the bejeweled watch bracelet to hold in her hands while she said a prayer to Camille in heaven.

Lily returned to the bank, and the manager quickly dropped what he was doing to rush out and greet her. "Bonjour, Mademoiselle Lily," he said as he looked at the young woman in front of him smartly dressed. Their business arrangement had been a good one, and he was more than pleased to work with the savvy woman working her way up the social ladder. With the loan almost paid off, he agreed to increase and extend it as she requested.

She had further goals ahead.

Lily became friends with owners of the café next door to the bakery, and in time, Lily offered them a payout so she could combine the businesses as well as the flat above the café that she turned into a tailor shop. Whether in hiring her staff or how she catered her business to clientele, she made sure to represent all classes, for she remembered the days when once she had little in the world. The tailor shop carried less expensive clothes to meet the needs of the middle and lower classes, but when she acquired the flat next to the tailor shop, she made it into a high-end boutique for the upper class. That really got things going for her. All of Paris's high society visited and purchased from her shop. Soon everyone in the city was talking about Lily and Lily's Boutique recognized for its fine service and quality.

She and her mother were continually invited to mingle with wealthy patrons or go to the opera and fancy balls. Lily knew where her roots were and where she had come from and had no illusions. On the other hand, her mother so enjoyed going to the extravaganzas, and Lily recognized it as part of a game to be played. But she mostly enjoyed a quiet night at home, sitting by the fireplace and reading a good story.

So as Lily said, it was a game of sorts, and they were at the top of it. They eventually bought the whole building on the street, encompassing different shops on the lower two levels and she and her mother living on the top floor. Parisians respected the Gauthier name, and life couldn't have been better. All of it started with gifts from a dying girl, Camille, watches enclosed in bracelets of fine gold and blue sapphires.

Time passed. Every night, Lily unwrapped the bejeweled watch bracelet to hold in her hands while she said a prayer to Camille in heaven.

After some years, Lily's mother passed away. Lily remained involved with her businesses and continued to meet with clients and merchant traders, but she had handed over day-to-day business responsibilities to a manager whom she had long employed and trusted. All bank loans had been satisfied, and she retained all four bracelets. She was well regarded as a person of substance in Paris. She decided she wanted help with housekeeping duties of her living quarters, which included the entire third floor. So, she put an ad in the paper and began interviews.

Lily found the one she was looking for, a plain looking woman of humble manner and lowly means. She reminded Lily of her own mother many years before. One morning after a year or so, hoping that perhaps there might be some additional work for her, the cleaning woman brought along her young daughter. "Of course," said Lily. "We'll find something for her to do".

Time passed. Every night, Lily unwrapped the four bejeweled watch bracelets to hold in her hands while she said a prayer to Camille in heaven.

ⓖⓖ ⓑⓑ

One day as Lily sat in her bedroom at her dressing table mirror, she heard a quiet knock at her door. Lily rose to answer it, and opening the door, she saw the little girl holding clean linens.

"Good morning, child" Lily said. "Why don't you just place those on the chest at the end of my bed?" Then she added, "Come over here and brush my hair."

As the little girl brushed, Lily asked, "What is your name child?" The young girl replied, "Camille."

Lily studied the reflection of the little girl's face behind her. "Of course you are," Lily said.

How perfect Lily thought to herself, knowing the name Camille in its French origin means perfect. And how perfect it is, thought Lily. Oh, so perfect.

"Do you see that watch enclosed in a bracelet of fine gold and blue sapphires on my dresser?" Lily asked the young girl.

The little girl nodded.

"Someday I will leave that to you as my gift to you, as it was once given to me. If you are ever in need of something important—food, clothes or a better place to live that you can't afford—you can sell it. It is worth a lot of money and will provide you some temporary comfort."

"I'd never sell it" replied the little girl, adding "I'd always keep it. I'll treasure it because it's from you." Lily smiled and, looking at the little face of the child, said "I was hoping you would say that."

And at that moment Lily realized that this was confirmation that perhaps Camille's legacy would continue on. And for how long? Perhaps indefinitely?

Lily then plainly stated, referencing a very special question, "Now stay with me a while and tell me all the favorite places you like to go to in Paris".

Excited, the little girl told Lily about her visits to the cabaret near the Montmartre with the red windmill on its roof, the Moulin Rouge. She was sometimes let in the side door by a doorman who befriended her, and she watched the can-can dancers and listened to the music and saw people there from all walks of life. There were artists, workers from the middle classes, businessmen, elegant women, and foreigners, too. It was such an exciting place, and in the gardens, the place even had an elephant. "And the next place I like to go to is . . . ."

Nothing more needs to be said
of Camille's legacy and where it had led,
for now the story is told and how it ends,
the story of Camille and Lily, two best friends.

The Bad Man with the Halo

I begin this tale of a man's life and plight.
His soul was darker than the blackest of night.
Nothing could be done to set it right
till God would have him in his sight.

It begins in a small hamlet down by the sea,
this story of a man and what would be.
Of what would happen, there would be no guarantee.
That much we know and all agree.

He was mean and nasty in every degree.
He cared for no one, and no friend had he.
He was sneaky and shady, within him no light.
He struggled through the world, try as he might.

He drank and cursed and cheated, too,
and with a needle to his arm he drew,
in ink so thick the color of blue,
the grinning devil—his proudest tattoo.

Oh, he was an evil man through and through,
and everyone in town was aware and knew
to stay away from him, for he was taboo.
Whenever he was close, they withdrew.

But then came the fateful day when he got sick,
and pain racked his body. It came so quick.
He tossed in his bed and became deathly ill
due to years of drinking that sapped his will,

and for the cruel life he'd made. That is where it had led:
alone not remembered on a solitary bed.
Nothing in the room—it was completely bare,
only him in the bed and no one to care.

He was weary of this life and his body broken
ever so long since he had last spoken.
Aware his life would be over before sunrise,
he lay his head down and closed his eyes.

Thus was the end that he knew,
but little he knew that he hadn't a clue,
because due to the way he had lived his life,
no peace would come yet—perhaps only strife.

He watched as his soul began to rise
and leave behind all its earthly ties.
As he rose in the sky to the heavens above,
what would be the fate for one so unloved?

Surrounded by blossoms and tree clusters of elm,
he arrived at the gates of the heavenly realm.
Angels were there but would not let him pass,
for they saw him for what he was, a snake in the grass.

Standing guard at the gate, they called for their Maker,
as it was God's decision to make, him the Creator.
The Almighty appeared, looked into that soul.
The man before him was bad, but he might have a role.

God spoke with wisdom in a voice of severity.
God offered a choice as he said with clarity,
"Your past was evil and surly, so to redeem your worth,
I'll offer you a way to have a chance for rebirth."

For God knew the man's trade had been on the sea,
and God had heard a calling, a desperate plea
from a young girl barely afloat
and barely alive in a small boat.

She was lost and alone in deep waters blue.
God said, "Listen well, for this is what you must do.
You must find that girl and bring her safely ashore,
back to land first, but then I request more.

"You must guide and teach her well of the seas,
so she will grow up with your skill and expertise.
As my messenger and servant, a halo shall ye wear.
But remember. I'm watching. So always beware.

"Treat the young girl with utmost respect.
Watch over her and see that you never neglect
till, with a trade and income as the result,
she's a woman no longer in need of your consult.

"You will stay by her side until I beckon.
Then I will decide your fate and how to reckon.
This is the quest I've decided you're in.
Be off now. I command you to begin."

And who knew better of the ways of men
to send the man out to redeem and amend?
The man was overwhelmed because then he knew
his soul might be cleansed if he did the work true.

Back to earth God sent him with wings to fly,
to achieve the holy mission he must abide by,
in hopes of a miracle like finding a pearl,
he went straight off in search of the girl.

He searched above waters and oceans so blue
for so long with no luck. What was he to do?
With feelings of discouragement and fatigue, too,
he questioned how he would see it through.

And then off in the distance on a white-capped wave,
he glimpsed a boat carrying a young girl so brave.
It was windy and stormy and looked so grave.
He battled the elements—with all his strength he gave.

He made it to the boat and began to row
as high winds picked up and began to blow.
He struggled with effort to keep the small boat upright,
and he looked around but saw no land in sight.

The young girl had been weeping, so lost in fright,
but then saw the man with a halo so bright.
He appeared out of nowhere into her boat,
and with his strength, he kept them afloat.

She knew not where he had come from,
but with joyful emotion, she was overcome,
for she knew she was not alone.
There was someone with her, though the man was unknown.

But she was not fearful, for it was a sign
that her plea to the Almighty, her prayer line,
to please save her and reach the shore,
had been answered. She'd worry no more.

Into the night, the man steered the boat,
and to keep her warm, he gave her his coat.
And when the rain came forth in a burst,
he collected it in his hat to quench their thirst.

Showing her their importance for what they provide,
he used the stars above as his compass and guide.
He gave her nuts from his pocket and caught fish with a hook
to satisfy her hunger and show her the skills it took.

Their path was decided as the morning came.
The seas became calmer, and she was the first to exclaim.
She pointed to the distance and the sight of land,
and as they rowed onward, the land continued to expand.

They beached their boat on a shoreline of sand
and looked around to see what was at hand.
They spied a small village and shepherds, too,
but not too close, which was best, they knew,

for although the girl could talk and see the man,
she was aware and knew keenly that no other can.
With plans in their heads to start anew,
they walked to a place with a beautiful view.

He built her a house of rock and stone
and remained close by so she wasn't alone.
During the calm days they set out to fish
and ate dinner together of that sweet dish.

When walking the beach, they collected kale,
then set for home with their fish to clean and scale.
Those things he taught her so she would know,
and she learned and listened as he told her so.

He planted a garden, and vegetables grew,
and together with fish she made a stew.
He taught her how to make utensils from bone,
and she practiced the skills she would hone.

He brought out fishing nets for them to mend,
and all other chores together they'd tend.
He even showed her how to fix a shoe,
thus, continuing and keeping his promise true.

She grew older until age seventeen.
She traveled to the village with the man unseen
to sell her goods and the fish she had gleaned,
the utensils she had made, their quality esteemed.

The villagers were curious but felt delight,
to have in their midst a young woman so bright.
"Who is this?" they asked. "Who provided that food?"
She cheered them with happiness and lightened their mood.

They welcomed her in, and soon everyone knew
that lovely young woman in her dress of blue,
and all the people accepted her bar none.
Her future there had then begun.

She gave a smile and a coin to street children less fortunate.
She was a good person, trustworthy and compassionate.
She said, "The people here accept me as one of their own,
and here I can sell my fish and utensils of bone."

When they returned back to their house by the sea,
she made herself and the man with the halo sweet tea.
She watched him as the day slowly changed to twilight
and thought about everything he had done so right.

He was mostly quiet except when giving guidance,
but she wondered what was behind his silence.
As she looked at the man with the halo sitting beside her,
she softly asked him her question in a quiet whisper,

"What happened to you, because sometimes you seem sad?"
He replied, "I may have a halo but I was once bad."
She gave him a kiss on his cheek and said,
looking into his eyes as she pled,
"Don't worry so much. Don't dwell on the wrong."
Then smiling, she lay back on the grass and sang him a song.

He thought to himself, *What creature is this so sincere and sweet,*
singing me a song on the grass by my feet
showing me kindness and caring, knowing our bond is deep?
And he knew for once in his life that feeling he would keep.

The man with the halo saw everything she did,
the opposite of everything in his first life that he hid.
To her he had passed on everything good he had known,
and she had become a woman fully grown.

She knew her time with him would soon be gone,
her time with the man who guided her and made her strong.
She would miss his presence and the memories they shared.
She thanked God for sending him, the God who cared.

As she sat beside the man with the halo on their last night,
she offered him thanks as she gazed into the moonlight.
"Someday I'll have a husband and children. I'll be his wife.
You've given me a blessing for a good and happy life."

And at that moment, a godly voice did sound,
"It is time to return. You are no longer earth bound."
God said, "You've kept your promise, as I shall to you.
So, return to me now. This I ask you to do."

God met him at the heavenly gates and ushered him in
and told the man he was absolved of all past sin.
For what the man had done in his second life,
God said, "This will be the end of your internal strife."

With beautiful thoughts at her home by the sea,
remembering the man with the halo and how it used to be.
She prayed and remembered why he was sent.
He had been with her a long time wherever she went,

for it felt he was hers, hers alone, she knew.
"You'll always be in my heart and my bond with you."
So, with a kiss farewell, her head she bowed,
praying, "You're not a bad man. You're a good man now."

She prayed that prayer to the man above,
the man with the halo who had been once unloved.
And every night to him that prayer she did send,
and that is how the story did end.

The Deity of Color

Their faces aghast with terror, their faces white as sheets,
the people ran all about, rushing through the streets.
Their eyes scanned all around and looked at the sky.
Confounded and confused were they hearing their children cry.

Everything was dark and grey, and no color in sight was shown,
as if black magic had appeared: it was like nothing ever known.
Lords in the castle gathered about, assembling there to talk.
Their voices showed their concern and their considerable shock.

"What happened to bring this about?" they asked, for it was so unclear.
Everyone in the castle hall was enveloped in total fear.
The king was up in his tower room, so what was he to do?
He was the only one they counted on, whom all royalty looked to.

Inside the room which was dimly lit by wavering candlelight,
the king was in his chamber with feelings so contrite
as he took up the pen with his hand and dabbed it in the ink,
then paused with a lingering sigh to momentarily rethink.

For he wanted just the right words before he began to write,
with feelings of regret and remorse and feelings revealing fright,
because he hadn't believed her before the words she informed
to him in the letter she had sent when she had forewarned.

So, what could he say at that point to make it all seem right,
for it was in the vision that she saw the one from her second sight,
the foretelling of a prophecy that had come to her in the night—
that Evil Shade would soon approach, arriving in black and white.

Its purpose and goal was to remove all color. That was its wicked plan,
ROY G BIV would never exist anymore once its quest began,
just differing shades of grey would remain and nothing else at all.
She had written of that in her letter to him in a hurried scrawl.

So, who was the one with the prophecy who wrote those eerie words
and then delivered to the king by her celestial shimmering birds?
For there is only one known, and of that we have few clues,
of the one whose duty it is to sprinkle our world with rainbow hues.

She was known as the Deity of Color giving us all such beautiful sights
to dazzle our eyes with brilliant spectrums filled with visual delights.
So now I'll tell you what I have been told about that one so divine
by one who claims to have seen her once in the sanctity of her shrine.

She wore long glass chandelier crystals that hung low from her ears,
and she held in each one of her hands circular kaleidoscopic spheres.
On her head, which glittered and sparkled, was a prismatic headdress,
and iridescent angels were at her feet all kneeling in faithfulness.

Continually sprinkling red and orange, yellow and green color, too,
and blue and indigo and violet colors is their commitment to do
so that everything we see all about us and through every season,
we are forever touched by them but without knowing the reason.

We take it for granted, don't we, not thinking of the "what if"—
if color were removed and disappeared in some sort of seismic shift.
Then everywhere one would see about, all would be dark and grey.
Every color that we had ever known, each would be taken away.

Well, that was how it came to be through the lands of the kingdom,
all due to the king's total ignorance and lack of judgment and wisdom.
So the king began to write his letter and ask her for her forgiveness,
as the commonfolk were so alarmed and beginning to be suspicious

of what had happened to their world. Was it coming to an end?
"What would the king do now?" they asked. "What savior could he send?"
He wrote exactly that request to the sparkling Deity of Color.
He asked who it was could save them as their visions grew duller.

She replied, "You must find the one they call the Lonely Reclusive Painter.
You'll find him living on top a mountain peak in a clear glass container.
My iridescent angels will accompany you as he is leery of strangers.
They will provide both direction and safety if you encounter any dangers."

The king had no idea why that man was the one he should seek.
How would some odd painter help? She replied he was unique.
Off the king and the angels traveled up high the mountain side,
and there at the peak beheld a sight. A glass pyramid they eyed.

A man in a smock in front of an easel—that is what they saw inside.
Blank canvas in front of him took shape as brushes of paint he applied.
The king then introduced himself as the angels all knelt nearby.
The painter continued to do his work but acknowledged, "I know why.

"I usually keep to myself up here away from all mankind,
but I know why you've come to me and why you're in a bind."
He clearly saw the angels there and knew it was a sign
that the request was really from the One, the one they call divine.

"They say my specialty is black and white and every shade thereof,
and I was taught by the Deity herself, the one from up above.
I also know what Evil Shade has done to take it all away.
I'll gladly track him down for you, and I will make him pay."

The king and the painter, made ready for their deadly trip
and led their horses down to the valley from the mountain tip.
They rode and rode and rode some more, the angels by their side,
until they reached a waterfall where they thought the Shade would hide.

They carefully made their way along a slippery, rocky ledge
behind the flowing water as it fell on the narrow edge.
Then coming to a darkened cavern behind a wall of spray,
they cautiously entered into it resolved to find their prey.

Deeper and deeper and deeper they went one careful step at a time.
The painter then whispered to the king. "Take this brush of mine."
He pulled another brush from his pack, and onward did they go,
paintbrush weapons in their hands to defeat their deadly foe.

They found the Shade behind a stone slab, and the angels made a spell,
to keep him unconscious while they did their work in the stony cell.
The painter removed paint from his pack and said, "This should do well."
They lathered the Shade's entire body with it, and then
they said, "Farewell."

The king could not understand it at all, why the deed would work.
No colors had he seen on the Shade till the painter said with a smirk,
"The Shade is one who cannot survive with color upon his being.
What we used was black-light fluorescent paint, so it seems unseen."

Then to the king's surprise, the painter turned on a black light
attached to the stony wall beside the Shade and at just the right height.
The king jumped back in alarm to see
bright psychedelic colors of every kind
encompassing the Shade's body as the image they left behind.

They hurriedly backtracked along their path,
from whence they had first come,
out of the cavern and watery ledge to wait for the Shade to succumb.
The Shade finally did awake to find himself covered in paint.
He struggled to make his way to the mirror. Fearful he would faint,

he screamed out when he saw himself all aglow. He knew what was in store
as he watched his reflection in the glass dissolving to puddles on the floor.
The king, the painter, and the angels saw, glad expressions on their face,
the wonderful world of colors returning, everywhere and in every space.

The people rejoiced throughout the land and in every place,
and children learned before each meal to say the following with their grace.
We thank the one responsible, the one divine unseen,
the Deity of Color, the one called Color Queen.
We give thanks for the visual delights she gives.
We know that only through her does true color live.

The Lost Child

I closed my eyes and then found myself in an unfamiliar place,
a circular building and room it was, only curved walls did I face,
for I stood alone in a rotunda with a dome high above my head,
and painted there on the ceiling, were flamingos by a river bed,

in an oasis filled with tall palm trees surrounded by sandy dunes.
And each bird wore a necklace of gold imbedded with magic runes.
Their S-shaped necks fine-feathered and each standing on one leg
in the middle a pyramid-shaped pedestal, on its top a golden egg.

As I wondered who had painted it and what all those images meant,
leaping through the windows came gazelles,
horns curved backwards and bent.
They skidded to a sudden halt when they saw me standing there.
Like frozen statues, not one of them moved, and all I could do was stare.

Then they all began to nibble away on low shrubs of butcher's broom,
ones that have false thorny leaves and small greenish flowers in bloom.
Most unusual it was, I thought to myself, but quickly there and then,
they zig-zagged as they frolicked and then back out the window again.

The floor design had a crisscross pattern made up of moss and stone,
and in the center of the rotunda, a white sculpture quite unknown
of a magnificent marble dragon, and I was enthralled with that sight
appearing so lifelike with wings spread and about to take to flight.

My fingers softly brushed the marble, tracing along its carved lines.
As I did, I felt a twinge of movement, a tingling sensation at times.
Was there something more to it, I thought, *than what I could comprehend?*
Or possibly something ahead for me, an outcome to portend?

The paths on the floor led to a door inscribed with unknown words
in a language unfamiliar and strange with symbols of creatures and birds.
I approached, and coming close enough, I pushed the door with my hands
to reveal a vision before me then of a life in a faraway land.

I saw a woman gently sobbing and a man attempting to console,
so I said not a word but listened closely, to hear their story whole.
They were from a desert tribe, Bedouins tried and true,
a hardy people they were indeed and stoic through and through.

But that day the women wailed in their goat- and sheep-hair tent.
Evidently they had lost their child. They didn't know where she went.
The child apparently played outside when a dust storm surprised them all.
In blinding sand with no clear vision, she didn't hear them call.

When the winds died down and finally subsided,
she was nowhere to be seen.
"Why" the women all cried out, "is this world so cruel and mean?"
They huddled together and prayed to God to listen to their plea.
I entered the tent and sat cross-legged. They took no notice of me,

but the tent became very solemn and quiet, all listening spellbound
when a fine frail, wispy voice said "Once I was lost and then found."
An elderly woman held up the child's toy, a small pink woven doll.
"This flamingo I hold here in my hand was her favorite one of all.

"The child told me flamingos protected her if ever she had the need,
but to find her again we must request help from another to succeed.
They tell tales of a great white beast that flies above us all,
that watches over all the ones who are weak, meek, or small.

"And there is someone among us right now, yet he is one unseen . . . "
Then looking at me directly, she said," . . . who stands in worlds between.
Find that white flying creature," she said to me, "to help us find our child."
Then she placed the flamingo doll at my feet, and with her eyes she smiled.

What is this that she said to me? I thought for I could not be heard.
And as most rose up to leave the tent, my reality became so blurred
as they walked by but also through me. I then grew acutely aware
that my presence was only a mystery, for I was not physically there.

I pondered what she had asked of me and what I was going to do.
I closed my eyes, and I was back at the door I had come through,
for I stood alone in a rotunda with a dome high above my head,
and painted there on the ceiling were flamingos by a river bed.

Knowing that he was the one, I purposely walked to the white dragon,
foretold in the old woman's tales, for the quest to be begun.
I again traced with my fingertips, and the statue opened its eyes.
The marble started to crumble away as it stretched and began to rise.

It opened its mouth with fiery breath and said "Who is it that you seek?"
I said, "I found myself in a desert tent, and of a lost child did they speak.
I'm searching for that small Bedouin girl, the one lost in a sandstorm.
They said you are the only one to help with this task I must perform."

The dragon breathed again and asked, "Are there any other details?"
I replied, "Only that the young girl spoke fondly of pink flamingo tales."
The dragon calmly replied to me, "I know precisely where she is.
Climb on my back, and I'll take you there to find the little miss."

Then we flew for many miles over drifting dunes of sand,
and as I spotted an oasis below, we circled and glided in to land.
I was shocked to find that we were in the painting on the ceiling.
Everything was then revealed in a sight so very appealing.

Flamingos watched as we approached, their heads all turned one way.
I felt I entered into the midst of one massive pink ballet
in an oasis filled with tall palm trees surrounded by sandy dunes,
and each bird wore a necklace of gold imbedded with magic runes,

their S-shaped necks fine-feathered and each standing on one leg
in the middle a pyramid shaped pedestal, on its top a golden egg.
The flamingos then all parted for us to leave an open path
leading to the golden egg in the middle of a cooling bath.

The flamingos all then bowed low as the dragon and I walked past.
To the dragon they whispered,
"Great White One, we've done as you have asked,
our fidelity always to keep lost ones safe until you leave your dome
and fly to our oasis here to return them back to their home."

I approached the egg and tapped on it, and as the gold shell peeled,
pieces began to crack and fall, and a little face was revealed.
It surely was the Bedouin girl looking back at us both
to say "I promised the flamingos to believe in their sacred oath.

"I trusted them I would be safe here in my lovely egg
till the great white winged one appeared. Now, take me home, I beg."
Then looked at me to say, "Are you lost, too, sir, another?"
"No," I replied. "I was sent to find you by request of your grandmother."

Her eyes grew wide when I said that. "Do you know her?" she asked.
I said. "Only when she called on me to accomplish a mysterious task."
The dragon stooped and picked her up, gently placing her by his neck.
I climbed on beside her, too. We held on tightly to begin our trek.

He flew till we saw the Bedouin tents coming up and into our view.
She exclaimed, "You, the dragon, and flamingos have made it all come true."
The dragon didn't want to be seen, of course, nor cause an undue fuss,
so he glided down behind a large sand dune, and
that was where he put us.

He said, "Take her home to her family there, just over that sandy drift,"
and placed a small white package in my hands. "And give her this gift."
We walked hand in hand, just the two of us, the small Bedouin girl and I,
and she turned and waved to the dragon to say "Thank you and good-bye!"

Her nomad family came out of their tents, running toward her, and wow—
all shouting and crying, thanking God and wondering how
the miracle that had happened to her and how she had ever returned,
though right then they didn't care about that as far as they were concerned.

All that mattered was she was back and safe as they gathered around her.
I ducked quietly into the sheepskin tent so
I could approach the grandmother.
I said to her, "This is a gift for the child from the great white-winged beast."
She replied, "She will find it on her sleeping mat after our thanking feast."

To me the elderly woman then said "I know you are not of this world,
but I think you were sent here on a purpose, so you were then swirled
into our dusty desert sand winds and then ultimately into our tent,
your mission to help save my granddaughter. You were heaven-sent.

"I know that no one else can see you, but I also know in my old bones
that there are those who have wandering lives in different reality zones."
I opened the flap and withdrew from the tent as the others entered in,
all of them ready and joyous, too, to let the celebration begin.

Then, that night, as the little girl went to her mat to sleep,
she found awaiting a small package there, a precious one to keep.
"Did the man give this to me?" she asked, looking at her grandmother.
The elder answered, "Other than the dragon,
are you saying there was another?"

"Yes," the girl replied. "The man who brought the dragon to save me.
He flew with me and held my hand. Grandmother, don't you see?"
"Yes, I saw him, child," said Grandmother,
"but I didn't know you could, too,
so we both have special powers, don't we? That I figured you knew."

They sat together on her mat as she opened up the gift.
She unwrapped the paper carefully, and as it started to lift,
saw inside a beautiful red veil with many coins that matched.
All hanging by numerous golden threads, they were all attached—

tiny flamingos and golden eggs and in the middle of them all,
a white medallion of a winged dragon engraved on a white golden ball.
Her grandmother said, "This is quite beautiful. You'll have it for your life,
"for with your trust in flamingos, child, you should have no further strife."

And lastly she said to her granddaughter
as they sat in their tent huddled together,
"A reminder it is of those, child, who helped you on your way—
the flamingos and the dragon and the man from far away."

Flight of the Ladybug

The young woman had arrived not long ago,
but she didn't know why she was there, and so,
she put on a brave face to appear unfazed.
Now follows an account of four of her days.

Day 1 • Summer

She wandered serenely enjoying her time.
She entered a greenhouse with moonflower vine.
She strolled through gardens with manicured lawns,
then to a round pond to observe its black swans.

Throughout the grounds stood statues of those long past.
Some were of children whose lives didn't last.
She stopped and contemplated why it was so.
What happened to them in times long ago?

She continued on to her favorite place.
As she drew closer, she felt a mist on her face
from fountain waters sprayed up high in the air.
She smiled and, with an appreciative stare,

lay down without a care on the nearby grass
and whiled away the hours to let the day pass.
She listened to sounds of water flow over
sculptures therein of dolphins with clover.

A Beetle of Our Lady with all its charm
landed ever so lightly upon her forearm.
The orange ladybug rested to its heart's content.
As the girl gazed wistfully, she knew its intent

to bring her good luck with a creative mind.
And she sighed and wished that for herself in kind.
Lying on her back looking up at the sky,
she watched cumulous clouds gently floating by.

She had wandering thoughts of what lay ahead.
At night she remembered when tucked in her bed
all the tomorrows to surely come her way
whatever happened. That day was a good day.

Day 2 • Fall

Rain pitter-pattered against her windowpane.
Her thoughts drifted away down memory lane
from her private chamber on that dreary day.
She peered out the window at the carriageway.

Their branches swaying with the wind to and fro,
graceful white birches lined all in a row,
shedding a golden carpet upon the road.
Sitting at her oak desk she hummed the same ode.

As music drifted from the parlor room suite,
"On an autumn day," a minstrel's voice sang sweet.
In front of her, she placed parchment and inkwell,
for that is where she would sit for quite a spell

considering what to write with quill in hand,
there in the manor house in a foreign land.
Though her future presumed her mother and wife,
that was not what she intended for her life.

Not knowing where to begin, she tapped her quill.
Was she resigned to swallow a bitter pill?
She turned to look at the mirror on the wall,
her face staring back—could she recall?

"Return to me," she murmured in a soft tone.
"Ladybug, ladybug, oh, where have you flown?"
Many changes and chances forever gone,
she stretched out her arm for it to land on.

But, alas, it never came, so she closed her eyes.
Sad and lonely verses were her lullabies,
for although that particular day was grey,
chalk it down to being a rainy fall day.

Day 3 • Winter

Determined to explore her midwinter treats,
she rubbed her eyes and threw off her bedsheets.
She felt a chill as she opened the shutters,
and tapering icicles hung from the gutters.

White ice crystals had formed on the panes,
frost weaving a design of spidery veins.
Wiping the glass, she could see fresh fallen snow.
She gazed out whispering, "I do love it so."

Bundled in a fur-lined coat, she rushed outside
breathing the crisp, clean air she felt so alive.
She turned her face upward as snowflakes kissed her skin.
What wondrous scenery to play a part in!

Nearby forest trees with their branches low,
all of them burdened with heavy snow,
each snowflake unique fell down from the sky.
Then just like that in the twinkling of an eye,

staring at her from the woods' edge stood a lynx
with a steady, intent look like a wise sphinx.
It moved cautiously toward her, then sat still.
"Don't be afraid," it said. "I come in goodwill.

"I have a message for you from someone close.
It's someone near and dear whom you love the most.
It's the ladybug who told me just one thing:
She will return back to you in the late spring."

The lynx leapt away and back into the wild.
She was overjoyed and, looking up, she smiled.
Maybe someone was watching her from above
on a special winter day, someone dearly beloved.

Day 4 • Spring
Flocks of honking geese flew north in formation.
Buds on tree branches began new creation.
Clusters of yellow daffodils grew in mounds,
and slim, white-leafed snowdrops peeped up from the grounds.

Daylight hours grew gradually longer in length,
and nature's rebirth displayed all its strength.
She rushed outside, took a breath, and settled down.
The marvels of God's gifts appeared all around.

Symbols of hope bordering the garden beds,
white snowdrops with their drooped, bell-shaped heads.
She focused on them and remembered the night
when an auspicious dream came to soothe her plight.

She would transform and then spirit away.
She longed for that time, that most special day,
for a year had passed, and she was still the same,
stuck in the manor in a waiting game.

She returned to her chamber to braid her hair.
She looked in the mirror and saw no one there.
Then a visible shape began to take form.
Her mind swirled, and her body was warm.

The image in the mirror, same as her thoughts
with wings, an orange body, and black spots—
her metamorphose to be what she would be—
a ladybug so she could be free.

She flew out through the window and then beyond
over black swans gliding below in their pond,
in the distance lush valleys and wooded dells.
That was when she said her parting farewells.

No one could find her in the morning dew
but saw her window had been broken through.
As patients gathered outside on their own,
they whispered to each other, "The ladybug has flown."

The Ultimate Sacrifice
Getting Ready For Battle

He began to prepare, for his mission so near
as he told her, "Don't worry. I'll return, my dear."
She removed her silk scarf and gave it to him.
"To keep and protect," she said proper and prim,

but inside dreading, thus feeling the worst
as she held his hands, into tears she burst.
They walked down the steps and into the light,
then before them they saw the gathering sight.

The king looked over from the keep balcony.
The lords and ladies watched from the gallery.
The pikemen and knights in the inner ward
then all bowed to the king, their grand earthly lord.

Swordsmen with shields and archers with bows
received his blessings to defeat their foe.
Her man would soon leave. He sat on his horse.
His armor was gleaming. His beard was coarse.

She gathered her skirts as her eyes looked up.
She offered him wine in a round, stirrup cup.
The trumpets then blared. The horses snorted.
Then tension grew as supply carts were sorted,

some for pots and tools and others, dried meat
and large bundles of hay and bushels of wheat.
For their encampment, many leather tents
and anything else needed. Carts carried those implements.

Squires hustled about attending the knights.
They would be so busy in the coming nights
helping with armor and attending the mounts.
Then all seemed to be ready, they did announce.

Knights and foot soldiers all started to move
out through both baileys their bravery to prove.
Sounds of feet stomping and clip-clops of horses
combined with crowd noise and the din of king's forces.

Their spirits were high. The crowds shouted out
all spurring them on, their enemies to flout.
Men at arms with their spears began to march.
The armed procession plodded under the arch

of the castle gates then across the drawbridge,
kicking up the dust as they went onto the ridge.
Their banners flew high, their colors were bright,
and then they grew smaller and soon out of sight.

She hurried from the courtyard for a better view.
On the battlement walls, a farewell kiss she blew,
knowing what lay ahead, the hardships to come.
Not all would return. Some would succumb.

The journey would be hard, but they'd all bear down
and battle their foes for the one wearing a crown.
She'd light candles for them for flames to protect.
Inside the chapel each night, that promise she kept.

Awaiting Word

As the months passed by, wild rumors were heard
of fantastic tales spoken, all unbelievably absurd,
that somehow the enemy was made up of ghosts,
as once dead avengers rose again from the coasts.

The king sent scouts to find out what they could
but when they returned it was understood
for as they approached the castle gates near
their bodies slumped over, and it became clear

an unfortunate fate for them was proved.
Their lives had been taken and their heads removed.
They returned dead to the castle, tied to their mounts.
At least that was told by all accounts.

Whispered by the citizenry, the story spread,
causing nightmares when they were tucked in bed.
Then, some brave souls were able to ride through
to find out what was and wasn't really true

about the king's royal army and what happened out there.
Those inside the castle all said a prayer
and hoped for the best, though doubts not to share,
they refused to speak openly. Would they ever dare?

Then messengers returned telling of their defeat,
their forces overpowered and in retreat.
The king in his castle was alarmed by the news.
"How could this be?" he asked. "How could we lose?"

Their Army Returns

They returned months later, beaten and battered,
their armor dented, and the men's blood spattered.
Looks upon their faces expressed agony of defeat,
some without weapons and rags on their feet.

They trudged dully and limping through the castle gates.
The remains of their army appeared in dire straits.
Last came carts carrying men who lost their limbs—
they neared painful death while confessing their sins.

Is my husband alive? is all she could think
as her heartbeat quickened and her hopes began to sink.
She searched the faces of the crowd coming in
till she saw one with her scarf and knew it was him.

He looked grave and exhausted and his face so thin,
unable to comprehend the courtyard chaos within.
She reached up to grab him, for he appeared dazed
as he looked down at her then with his eyes so glazed.

She helped him to the keep and into their chamber.
He lay on the bed, where he stayed the remainder
of that awful day. He recuperated and rested,
while she waited by his bedside as he had suggested.

Her holy beads in hand, she counted her blessings,
not knowing what had happened but only guessing
and thankful that he returned. For he had come back,
and by the grace of God, he had survived the attack.

The Tale of Their Defeat

The lords and the king gathered all in the great hall
to understand what had happened, once and for all.
Soldiers knelt before them with their story to tell
as she stood and listened intently near the stairwell,

"Many battles they fought, the enemy retreated.
Our leaders were confident the enemy would be defeated.
Our forces were pushing them back to the coast.
Our soldiers felt emboldened with victories to boast.

"We had driven them back. and then we reached the cliffs
as high winds howled and clouds had rifts.
We drove them all off the edges and then into the sea
down to the rocks below, their deaths to be.

"Then we all stood shouting, 'Long live the king,'
when we heard the outcome, good news to bring.
Victory was ours, and our emotions ran high
as we camped out that night under a dark, starry sky.

"Then hell and fury descended upon us that night,
for the sentries posted ran away in fright."
"Why did they all run away?" the king wanted to know.
The soldiers replied, and fear in their faces showed.

"Because the foes slain before came alive again.
Then nothing more to say, for how could you explain
where the enemy came from silently and undetected?
We were unprepared and the attack so unexpected—

"for before, our enemies' bodies lay stiff and prone.
But then they all began to rise as specters unknown,
wave upon wave attacking us with no mercy shown,
striking our soldiers deftly down, all their fates to own.

"Then our forces broke ranks, and chaos ensued.
We scattered and retreated, dragging our wounded, too.
Then, months of skirmishes as we made our way back
and fewer of us able to thwart any attack."

The king eased back in his throne, and all were silent
till at last he spoke up with his specific requirement.
"Go fetch the royal wizard, for what had he once said,
his vision of a do-or-die battle with an army of dead."

The Wizard's Advice

The wizard came in and observed all who were there.
He made his way into the room and was very aware
that all eyes were on him, their breath held in anticipation,
for they revered him as a prophet, such was his station.

Sitting at a table, he reviewed parchment scrolls.
They retold battle scenes of once-dead souls.
The story then finished, and he knew what was ahead,
the time had finally arrived. It was one he most dreaded.

"Only one I know has the power to raise up the dead.
To appease his anger, we'll offer a hostage instead.
It must be someone from court with royal blood,
but what their fate will be, I do not know," he shrugged.

"While we negotiate this, we must find what he wants,
or we'll never be rid the scourge, this being that haunts.
Otherwise, we'll all be crushed and on our bended knees.
And he'll have our heads, these written scrolls guarantee.

"For until we have a savior, there can be no rest.
Is there anyone here, my king, to take on this request?"
The lady by the stairwell waited while straining to hear,
but no one made a peep. They were overcome by their fear.

Was there not one among them, with the will to be brave,
to know that that sacrifice their kingdom would save?
None said they were for it nor said they opposed,
only total silence in the hall for what he proposed.

The lady by the stairwell, her heart pounding her breast,
stepped forward and announced, "I will at your behest."
Everyone was shocked by it, but the wizard had a grin.
Rising up, he spoke, "A better choice could not have been."

The Secret Agreement

He instructed her to follow him up to his tower chamber
where they could have a private talk: he asked as a favor.
He unlocked a door and bade her, "Come in to my abode,
for what I tell you is secret for one with a heavy load.

"Sit and listen to me carefully, as I'll tell it to you straight,
for this path you take forward will determine your fate.
No one else will ever know the plan we will devise.
You will go under false pretense, a hostage in disguise.

"I tell you, you will not be that, for an assassin you will be.
This is our only chance. Please act and set us all free.
I will give you a poison, powder to blow in his eyes,
but be aware that when it's done, there is no compromise."

The wizard hesitated but began again with a heavy sigh,
"But you will also breathe powder, so both of you will die."
He waited and watched her to see what she would say.
She then softly replied, "Well, then this shall be the way."

Her Departure

The people gathered together by the castle gates
to see her off with prayers, for in her hands were their fates—
a hostage, they all thought, but still wondered, Why her?
Final instructions in her ear gave the wizard whisperer.

Her husband, bewildered, asked "Why must it be you?"
She replied, "Always remember that our love is so true."
And then she was gone, galloping away on her horse,
for that was how it had to be, her destiny course.

The Aftermath

It was the last time they saw her, as she never returned.
But then tales were told. The specter's eyes had burned,
he and his undead army gone, ending their terror reign,
never seen or heard of again. That they couldn't explain.

All the people began again normal routines day by day,
    all the people and their king living in a carefree way
but for the one on his balcony. He would never forget.
    The wizard stood with his white dove by the parapet.

They say that every so often, you may see one from afar
    on the ridge beyond the castle walls, underneath a star,
    on a horse a woman staring wistfully toward the castle
    as all those inside continue with festivities to bedazzle.

She gave her life for her loved ones, her land, and her king.
    She would never be forgotten, the minstrels would sing.

The Mystic

She went to see the mystic to ask, "What is the meaning of our life?"
He said "First, you must experience things like love, joy, grief, and strife
for how you handle each one of them will determine your life and path
and which direction you decide to take it will show in its aftermath.

"To seek the signs that guide you along, be attentive to all of those.
The first step is to clear your mind, then meditate on what it shows.
Think about the words I've said, then return and I'll tell you more.
Perhaps you'll see things in your thoughts and why and what they're for."

She traveled back down the mountainside till she reached the land below
and found the perfect spot to contemplate
under a large willow tree shadow,
but then before she could settle her mind, she was distracted by a crow.
And the oddest thing about that one, it had one red feather aglow.

The feather was radiant and shimmering with a sparkling shine of light.
She stood and called out to say "Hello," for indeed it was a beautiful sight.
The crow flew down to land at her feet, then hopped up on her arm
and said "Don't be worried or frightful. I wish only to give you a charm."

It plucked off the lustrous red feather and placed it in her hand.
"It will help you in your journeys, the ones yet unseen and unplanned.
And if you feel you are ever in doubt, just rub the feather to see
the right paths and directions for your life revealed in clarity."

She climbed back up the mountain to see the mystic in his cave
to show him the radiant red feather and relay the message the crow gave.
The mystic pondered it over, then said, "So far, you've done well, child,
for to receive a gift like that is a sign the God above must have smiled."

She asked, "Teacher, if I go down the wrong path, I'll make mistakes. But
doesn't one learn from mistakes?"
"That is true," he said, "but whichever path you take will not eliminate
mistakes, for they are part of the learning process in life. However, when you
come to a fork in the road and take the wrong path, it is like taking a detour
that could put you or others in jeopardy. It takes time to get yourself back on
the right path. So the feather will help guide you in the correct direction to
always keep you moving forward, not backwards and then forward.
"Do you understand child?"
"Yes, teacher," she said.

The mystic said,
"So now you have a key to keep, to use to proceed correctly on your way.
Now think about how you would react to things that
happen on any particular day,
things that happen out of our control, things we don't even understand,
and when you've thought it over, then your knowledge should expand."

She traveled back down the mountainside till she reached the land below
and found the perfect spot to contemplate under
a large willow tree shadow.
At that moment, a small fox appeared from out the nearby brush.
She didn't want to scare it away, so she silenced her mind with a hush.

It came walking right up and put its nose to her hand.

To it, it gave a nudge,

and with its tongue, it licked its toe to remove any dirt or smudge,

and to her surprise revealed a claw of pure ivory, brilliant white.

The claw was radiant and shimmering with a sparkling shine of light.

It pulled the claw out from its paw and said,

"To help you when times are tough,

I give this gift, and if you rub the claw, I'm very sure it will be enough,

for perhaps what may occur ahead for you

may be terrible and tough to bear.

You might not like some things that will happen,

but at least you'll be aware.

You'll understand the reason why they occurred, for that will be the key.

It will soothe and ease your pain and grief or any strife that comes to be."

She climbed back up the mountain again to see the mystic in his cave

to show him the brilliant ivory claw and relay the message the fox gave.

The mystic pondered it over, then said, "So far, you've done well, child,

for to receive a gift like that is a sign the God above must have smiled."

She asked, "Teacher, aren't pain and grief a part of life?

Don't you learn things from going through difficult times?"

"That is true," he said, "but sometimes,

one may be overpowered by the emotions of grief, and when that happens,

it may take a long time before one becomes whole again or

may question why it happened.

The claw will not prevent suffering, but it will soothe the ache and provide

the inner strength to endure.

Do you understand child?"

"Yes, teacher," she said.

The mystic said,
"So now you have a key to keep, to use to proceed correctly on your way.
Now think about having material goods, an abundance of wealth someday.
Would you be the same person as now or one changed by that outcome?
Go ponder those things I've told you about, and determine the final sum."

She traveled back down the mountainside till she reached the land below
and found the perfect spot to contemplate under
a large willow tree shadow.
Just then, a magic jackalope came into view, part jackrabbit, part antelope.
He hopped and nestled beside her side while holding an envelope.

He blinked his eyes and said, "I offer a special gift for you,
a piece of my magical antler to help you see your journey through."
She opened up the envelope and was surprised to see inside
a tip of antler made both light and
strong from titanium with carbide applied.

The piece was radiant and shimmering with a sparkling shine of light.
He said, "Whenever you feel you're fortunate,
think of those who may be in plight.
For there is no better reason for giving and to do what you know is right.
You must be modest and unpretentious. in return you will gain insight.

"Money and many possessions in life are just a temporary delight,
but they are things you can't take with you
when your soul soars off to flight.
When you're undecided of what to do and to take the proper course,
just rub the antler with your hand, and it will be your guiding source."

She climbed back up the mountain again to see the mystic in his cave
to show him the brilliant antler piece and
relay the message the jackalope gave.
The mystic pondered it over, then said, "So far, you've done well child,
for to receive a gift like that is a sign the God above must have smiled."

She asked, "Teacher, if I had large sums of money,
couldn't I do a lot of good with it?"
"That is true," he said, "but one can also do good without money.
Money is not the end-all in the path of life. Money cannot ensure
happiness. Some are swayed by the pursuit of it, and it sullies the soul.
The purpose is not what you have, but what you leave behind.
The antler will help you to do what's right.
Do you understand, child?"
"Yes, teacher," she said.

The mystic said,
"So now you have a key to keep to use to proceed correctly on your way.
Lastly, we must think about joy and love,
but not as something to lead you astray.
Whether they be obsession or pleasure,
they would ultimately make you their prey.
Go and seek the meaning and how those two may interplay."

She traveled back down the mountainside till she reached the land below,
and found the perfect spot to contemplate under
a large willow tree shadow,
but then a leopard covered with beautiful spots appeared within her sight.

As it approached and opened its mouth, it said, "I mean to cause no fright,
for you are the one I've been looking for, and a gift I have brought for you
so you find and understand joy and love,
the emotions of those special two."
It pried open his jaw and, with its paws, pulled out a tooth from its gum.
It wasn't exactly the color of purple but more like a fluorescent plum.

The tooth was radiant and shimmering with a sparkling shine of light.
The leopard said, "This will tell you the one to choose,
the right time for you to unite.
They say love can be a fickle thing, and sometimes love can be blind,
but when love and joy are bound together as one,
then the bond is truly aligned.

"For what those special ones in your life
can bring to complete your other half,
gladly giving of themselves to you all for betterment on your behalf,
and show your love to others as well, and
true enlightenment will come through.
Rub the tooth, and it will show,
for the love you give is just as important, too."

She climbed back up the mountain again to see the mystic in his cave,
to show him the brilliant plum tooth and
relay the message the leopard gave.
The mystic pondered it over, then said, "So far, you've done well, child,
for to give you a gift like that is a sign the God above must have smiled."

She asked, "Teacher, love sounds good. Is it ever bad?"
"That is true," he said, "both good and bad. Bad when love becomes an obsession for someone or something, it will sour a relationship or cause misery in addiction. Good when you find a passion for something important to you or when giving loving care to those in need. It's to have someone in your life who means so much that you want them always to be with you to experience life with.
Ultimately, you have to love yourself. The tooth will help guide you.
"Do you understand child?"
"Yes, teacher," she said.

The mystic said, "Now you have received the lessons to help you in life's journey. If you use your gifts wisely you will gain meaning for your life. Teach others, as well, so they may find
a truer path for themselves.
God be with you, child.
Follow your path, for you are ready."

The Red Feather
The right paths and directions for your life will be revealed in clarity.

The Ivory Claw
It will soothe and ease your pain and grief or any strife that comes to be.

The Titanium Carbide Antler
Think of those who may be in plight,
for there is no better reason for giving.

The Fluorescent Plum Tooth
For what those special ones in your life can bring to complete
your other half.

The Three Golden Keys

Over the hills and over the vales,
you'll find a land of many tales
of their history and legends and wars they fought,
of treasures and riches that were lost and sought,
of princes and heroes and large armies they led,
of their courage and bravery and blood that was shed,
of ships on the oceans and serpents in the seas,
of wizards and magic spells that brought men to their knees,
of sorrow and sickness and lives wrought with strife,
of great kings and queens and royal life,
of cold winter nights and hard times endured
but also of good times with happiness secured—
of treachery, lies, and scoundrels as well.
Those are all in the stories the bards do tell.

But one I bring forward with much delight,
one special story I'll bring to the light:
a fair maiden walking with flowers in her hair
alone in the fields while leading her mare.

Her dress billowed in the brisk meadow breeze,
and attached on her belt were three golden keys.
What was so special of those keys of gold?
Have you not heard of the tale that is told?

It is passed down from generations of old.
'tis said a wish would be granted for each one you hold.
The maiden was seeking the one considered a sage.
She was seeking a woman of wisdom and old age.

She came to a village where they said she would be
and entered the sage's hovel. The sage offered her tea.
The sage told her, "Look into the cup. and you will see,
for that wish that you seek is where it will be.

"But promise me first what you will do for me.
You must give me a single golden key."
The maiden stared into her cup of tea
and saw her future and what was to be.

She saw a young man revealed who would capture her heart
and imagined her life with his, never to part.
She offered up the golden key that rested in her palm.
The sage smiled slightly but remained otherwise calm.

The maiden knew in her heart—so certain was she,
that she must find the man disclosed for her destiny.
She knew without doubt that he was her true love
while the sage took the key and tucked it into her glove.

The maiden rose and then saddled her mare
with much anticipation, not a moment to spare
with thoughts of the man and a life she would share
and knowing few in life find a love so rare.

She rode her mare to the castle in the distance
with determination and fervor—such was her insistence.
She arrived at the gates and threw down the mare's reins.
She hurried quickly through the streets and up through the lanes,

for she knew the man revealed was the son of the king,
and she needed the king's favor for the news she would bring.
As the guards unlocked and opened huge wooden doors,
she was struck by the beauty inside of bright marble floors.

With permission granted, she walked the royal halls
viewing ornate tapestries along the way adorning the walls.
She entered the main chamber and saw up ahead
the king and his joker and the prince she would wed.

Attempting to juggle and trying to sing
the joker was sprawled in front of the king,
and next to the king was the man revealed,
the one she hoped with her fate would soon be sealed.

She knelt in front of them to present her intent
and told her tale of her vision hoping for their consent.
The prince knew in that instant, though he had never seen her before,
facing him stood the maiden he had waited and longed for.

'twas as the histories foretold in royal scrolls of lore.
He need search no longer, his yearning erased forevermore.
For he knew she was the one destined to be and his heart to adore.
He said to his father, "I want to marry this maiden. I need no more."
And of his declaration to that he swore.

The king heard his son's words and was unable to dissuade,
for the prince's determination was already made,
but the king announced that a price must be paid,
for he slyly saw the golden keys on her belt as a trade.

He said, "I will grant you this marriage if you pay with a key,"
which the maiden offered up as the guarantee
for the two lovers satisfied and together at last—
everything they had hoped for, everything they had asked.

But the agreement would all be a ruse,
for the king wanted both keys—not one, but two.

The king gathered counsel, for the marriage could not be.
They devised a plan to enact to meet the king's plea,
a plan so evil and devious indeed
to be carried out secretly, for it to succeed.

They knew the maiden was not of royal blood line.
They schemed she would be poisoned by placing it in her wine.
That night, she was alone waiting in her room,
unaware of the impending doom.

A castle servant delivered her wine,
the maiden unaware of any deadly sign.
Though you may think this the end of our story line,
many more events that evening were about to intertwine,

for at that moment she heard a knock on her door.
In came her prince to hold her and their hearts to soar,
their eyes meeting each other as if in a stare,
so happy they were of their love affair.

But when she was busy putting rouge on her lips,
the prince opened the bottle and took the first sips.
As he fell choking and gasping to breathe,
trickling from his mouth liquid foamed and seethed.

The castle stirred as it heard of the news.
There were shouts and screams as all were confused,
that someone had taken the one held so dear.
The maiden was aware of her own fear,
that the poison had been for her: that's why it was placed there.

She would be blamed, that she knew.
She had to escape, and that she would do.
She gathered her strength to climb to the windowsill
and dove into the waters below, their depths so chill.

She mounted her mare and rode through the night,
without looking back till she was out of sight.
Her world was shattered, the reality not understood,
but then she resolved to do whatever she could.

For after receiving news that the young Prince was buried,
she went to that place with tools and garments she carried.
She dug in the dirt and pulled his body out,
wrapped him in fine cloaks—she had no doubt.

She draped him over her mare and started her trek
to the village on the horizon that appeared as a speck.
She thought again of the sage and what might be done.
Her heartbreak enormous, she knew the sage was the one.

She lowered her head as she entered the dwelling,
the maiden's tears falling as she told the retelling.
The sage then began with chants of expelling
and continued after with chants of dispelling.

The old sage placed the maiden's hands on her
and explained the magic she required for the transfer.
She then looked into her eyes as she said,
"This is what I must do to undead the dead.

"But once again a promise you must make to me.
You must agree to give me your last golden key."

The sage placed her hands on the prince's body and chased away death.
Then they both watched as the prince took a first breath.
Watching in awe as all was put right,
the maiden was astounded at the sight.

The prince rose and held his maiden near,
their love so full, their love so dear.
Knowing the bliss their future would be,
she gave up her third and final key.

Then they climbed on the mare ready to flee
over hills and vales and perhaps over the sea,
two lovers together so happy and free,
recalling the wonders brought by three golden keys.

The Magic Pill

The man was exhausted and his wife in constant tears,
as they watched over their daughter and suppressed their fears,
knowing their only child was succumbing to illness
and nothing they could do in the absolute stillness.

The husband sighed, sitting in his chair closing his eyes.
The sun had gone down—only a redness in the skies.
He felt so hopeless and overcome with sadness.
He dozed thinking maybe a method in this madness.

He received a vision, a purpose, sent from above,
so he went toward it following a white dove.
An angel greeted him and requested his assistance:
rising from the mist he saw towers in the distance.

The angel would say no more, he knew that for a fact.
He said he would consent, acknowledging their pact.
Heavy snow fell deep, and winds howled as they set forth.
Following the angel, he plodded toward the north.

He wrapped his cloak tightly to keep out freezing cold
while thinking of the angel, its eyes were flecked with gold.
They crossed rugged terrain and over narrow frozen streams
to the castle ahead he'd seen before in his dreams.

Two Minotaurs holding spears greeted them at the gates,
and said, "You are expected, but there've been no updates.
Follow the goat. He will lead you there. They await you."
He thought, *Alas, what have I gotten myself into?*

As the gates opened, they were met by a silver goat,
that led them to a stone bridge above a frozen moat.
On the ice below, young women glided by on skates.
Each held blue umbrellas while they did figure eights.

Crossing over the bridge, he stood before an archway.
Enormous castle walls above took his breath away.
The entrance beneath had thick ivy on its side walls
as the angel said to him, "This is where duty calls."

He entered the inner bailey where people gawked and thought,
Who is this mysterious man the heavens have brought?
Hoping his arrival there would bring them better days,
they murmured softly with blessings full of praise,

for all were worried about the precious little girl,
the one who had become ill, the daughter of the earl.
The goat led them to the keep, then up the winding stairs—
at the top a dark room full of people saying prayers

and lying on the bed before them, a child so pale.
The angel said, "What they've done has been to no avail."
The earl was at the bedside holding the child's cold hand,
and a wizard stood holding an hourglass filled with sand.

The man was baffled. *Was this why he had been brought here?*
He knew nothing of medicine to help the poor dear.
The man said, "I don't know how to treat someone who's ill."
The wizard smiled, saying, "We know, but you fit the bill."

The man looked around for the angel, but she wasn't there—
no longer beside him, vanished into thin air.
Then everyone in the room cried out in unison,
"You're to find the magic pill, and come back when you're done."

The wizard motioned by hand, and a portal took shape.
The man stood frozen and staring with his mouth agape.
The wizard said, "Here's your access and egress to take.
But you must return with the pill and make no mistake.

"There's no time to dilly-dally and fiddle around."
The wizard paused and turned the hourglass upside down.
"When the sand all passes it will be the child's last breath.
So what you do, sir, will determine her life or death."

Everyone shoved and pushed him toward the swirling gate,
saying "Find the pill and return before it's too late."
What could he do? He was just a man, a mere mortal
lost in his own thoughts as he stepped into the portal.

Before him were billowy clouds and the angel, too,
who said, "I'm sorry for not accompanying you through.
But there was much to prepare before your arrival,
and we must do what we can for the girls survival."

The angel led him toward the end of a long line
where people awaited the judgment from one divine.
She said, "You've been granted a meeting with the wise owl,
the issuer of miracles, so ignore his scowl,

"for he determines who does and doesn't receive them
with power to deny or give the miracle gem.
You can tell him your story, but just so you're aware,
not everyone will receive one, as there're few to spare."

He watched as people spoke to the owl, and when they left,
noticed some relieved but others weeping and bereft.
He became nervous and anxious, as his turn was next.
Then he stood in front of the owl and gave his respects.

The bespectacled owl sat hunched over a large desk,
two angels behind him dignified and statuesque.
Peering over his glasses asked, "Who do you speak for?"
The man said, "I'm here for a little girl at death's door."

The owl replied, "Well, I've heard all these sad tales before.
What can you tell me that's different to touch my core?"
The man told him, "In a dream, I walked through a blizzard—
led by a good angel to a castle and wizard,

"to a room where an earl's daughter lay sick in her bed.
I was pushed through a portal, my road ahead,
to find a magic pill to save her life was my due.
Now I stand across the table to ask that of you."

The owl was amused "A small girl in a dream you say?
I'll admit I don't hear requests like that every day.
I've never heard of a miracle for a dream child.
If that is what you're asking, this request should be filed!"

The man's angel stepped forward. "Owl, I asked for his help,
and he followed me willingly just like a young whelp.
He never questioned my motives. Determined was he
to save the earl's daughter from death, so helpless was she."

"Indeed?" The owl winked. "Miracles needed in all places—
perhaps in otherworldly dimensional spaces?
Angels are only sent out for those special cases,
to see and watch, thus covering all the bases.

"Come closer, young man, to receive what you came here for,
kissed by the lips of God and blessed in heavenly lore."
As he looked at the pill, the man asked, "She won't succumb?"
The owl laughed. "Believe me it'll do the trick and then some."

The man thanked both the angel and the owl profusely.
She took him to the portal and said, "Now go, quickly."
He emerged back into the dark castle chamber room,
but the atmosphere within was filled with gloom and doom.

"You're too late," said the wizard holding up the hourglass.
All the sand had sifted through. "What we feared came to pass."
The man looked at the little girl and rushed to her bed.
It couldn't have happened to her. She couldn't be dead.

The earl consoled him, saying "I know you tried your best."
Both were aware, seeing no breathing from her chest.
But what happened next astounded and shocked them all.
The man sat on the bed with his back against the wall.

He held her body in his arms and tilted her head back
and put his finger in her mouth to open it a crack.
He reached into his pocket and, holding her head still,
he dropped something down her throat. It was the magic pill.

All in the room silently watched the spectacle,
but nothing happened, nothing at all detectable.
People murmured and fidgeted there in the dim light.
All of a sudden, the little girl sat bolt upright.

She gasped, opening her eyes and breathing very fast.
The earl hugged the wizard. "She's returned to us at last."
Everyone was astonished at what had taken place.
The earl approached the man and said, "You're our saving grace."

Accepting congratulations from all those around,
the man bid farewell and entered the courtyard ground.
A woman ran through the crowd and shook him, yelling "Earle!"
He was justly confused, his mind and thoughts in a swirl.

"Earle, wake up!" As he did, he saw his wife standing there.
"You fell asleep," she said, her hand stroking his hair.
He was back home, sitting in his chair. But so afraid.
Afraid something bad had happened. Hope began to fade.

His heart sank as he saw tears streaming down her face,
and she said, "You won't believe it" as they locked in embrace.
"Our daughter is awake and has been asking for you.
A miracle, Earle. The fever's broken. She's come through."

He rushed to his child to find her sitting up in bed.
She smiled. He knelt down to kiss her, and she softly said,
"I want my two favorite toys close to me tonight."
From the shelf, he took the items that gave her delight.

One he had whittled and painted, a wood silver goat—
beside it, her snow globe, a girl in a winter coat
holding a blue umbrella while she skated on ice,
every detail of it meticulously precise.

As he stood at the foot of her bed, he wondered still,
had he witnessed a miracle of God's plan and will
or was it the angel who shepherded him until
he found what he had been searching for—the magic pill?

Shapeshifter and Skinwalker

Elders sat cross-legged in a circle so as to smoke
the hookah with flexible tubes. They would toke,
drawing in puffs and relaying stories to invoke.
The following is one tale of which they spoke,

an occurrence like it unimaginable and dreamlike.
Two girls were born at the same time and alike.
They were born in the same village atop hilly hills
in a place of wild golden lemon thyme and daffodils.

Identical in every way and looked just like the other,
for they were twins, but not from the same mother.
As the villagers awaited their arrival, they were told
the two infants born had future tales to unfold.

The people were aware of them as magic to protect,
so to guard the village, they began to erect
iron gates adorned with brass peacocks to ward off any
who might try to do them harm in that land of tyranny.

But rumors began to spread, and questions did arise.
Outsiders started to ask themselves, "Were they lies?"
as stories of what the girls could do were being told—
some said they were werewolves from a past of old

that would come in the dead of night and terrorize.
Others told of their eerie looks and their snake eyes
while others said they both had power to hypnotize,
but I'll tell you now the truths, so as not to fantasize.

Sofia was the one everyone called Shapeshifter,
always able to change form and identity in a flicker.
She could change herself into anything she wanted
but never an instance when it was show or flaunted.

And Sadie was the one everyone called Skinwalker,
for she was the quiet one, not much of a talker.
Sadie could possess or disguise into any animal
by entering their skins and minds swift and casual.

Decide for yourselves what future actions imply,
for it is without a doubt something went awry.
The tales of both the Shapeshifter and Skinwalker
and whether they're being stalked or being the stalker.

Everything was calm till the king wanted them dead.
He had heard the rumors as tales of the two spread,
bizarre stories being told through the land, he knew.
So he invited them to court to see if they were true.

Sofia and Sadie were escorted to the castle.
He commanded they show him something to dazzle.
Sofia turned herself into a flowering tree with fruit.
Sadie transformed into a chimpanzee playing a flute.

Everyone laughed and clapped at the display.
The demonstration so innocent was that little soiree,
the king nodded approval but was much more wise.
He knew what they did in trying to disguise

the real powers they might possess and which
would be his undoing, so in a voice with a high pitch,
he told his guards to arrest them and lock them in chains
and throw them in the dungeon for giving him migraines.

The two had been tricked, but neither was surprised.
They drew upon their powers, the ones they devised.
Sofia turned into a snake to slither and slide,
Sadie into a mouse riding her back to the other side,

escaping through the bars of the cell door, and then
slithering through castle halls to freedom again.
Outside the castle walls, Sofia turned into a bird.
Sadie, the mouse, hopped on without saying a word,

and the two flew off into the sunset very free.
For Shapeshifter and Skinwalker, it was meant to be.
When their escape was discovered, the king roared,
"I want their heads on a platter. I will not be ignored."

He ordered his soldiers to search lands everywhere—
not to return until they had destroyed that pair,
no quarter shown to anyone and no mercy spared
until Shapeshifter and Skinwalker were ensnared.

The king's soldiers came swiftly in the dead of night.
They held their torches high on horseback for light,
for they had tracked them to the village atop hilly hills,
the place of wild golden lemon thyme and daffodils.

They woke up the villagers and scared them that night
to declare the king's decree with power to extradite,
for by hook or by crook or come hell or high water,
they badly wanted Shapeshifter and Skinwalker.

Anxious to catch them before they could take flight,
they asked the common folk, "Has there been any sight?"
No answer from the villagers, who kept their lips tight.
The two concealed themselves and would be alright,

managing somehow or other or one way or another
their magic ritual to conjure and their state to alter,
Sadie became a horned beast, holding fire to ignite.
Sofia became the wind and blew with all her might.

They came from out of their hiding in light so bright,
frightening wind and fire, merging to become white
directly on the soldiers till all dissipated into a mist.
Nothing remained with their horses dismissed.

Sofia and Sadie went back to girls again with a twist,
for on the road ahead lay adventures not to be missed.
Taking only one path forward which led to the king,
the perfect end to him the two would bring.

The king was furious when told of the news—
how the two escaped his soldiers. He hated the ruse.
And then other soldiers were leery to confront,
for they heard the story of others in the hunt

who vanished mysteriously after confronting them.
Were Shapeshifter and Skinwalker causing mayhem?
All soldiers sent searching the king did seek.
Only their horses returned with empty saddle seats.

So the king enticed mercenaries with purses of gold,
to put an end to the madness of the two, oh, so bold.
But nothing he did could stop them from their goal
as they arrived to reclaim everything he stole.

So he sweated and waited with guards at the gates,
the end drawing nearer to determine their fates.
He placed guards along the walls and the towers
and also by his chamber door while his mood soured

with Sofia and Sadie, Shapeshifter and Skinwalker,
no longer being stalked but become stalkers.
As they drew near the castle, Sadie changed into a cat.
Their plan in place gave no time to chitchat

as Sofia became a black widow with deadly toxin.
The cat, spider on its back, proceeded with caution,
crossing the moat and climbing the walls with claws.
They reached the king's chamber windowsill and paused.

The cat leaned by the edge as the spider crept inside,
scurrying along the floor and then up to the bedside
where the king slept soundly with no clue
to what Sofia the Shapeshifter was just about to do.

The spider slowly crept till it reached the king's neck
to deliver a deadly poison bite, and then, like a speck,
returned to the windowsill to attach to the cat's back.
Down the castle walls, the cat gripped the stone cracks

till they reached the moat and then further away,
their mission accomplished. Nothing more to say.
Back they went to the village atop hilly hills,
the place of wild golden lemon thyme and daffodils.

They heard the king was deathly ill and had a flutter,
then silenced forever with naught further to utter.
Throughout the land, people rejoiced and exclaimed,
thanking who brought it about. The two unnamed

managed somehow or other or one way or another
their magic ritual to conjure and their states to alter.
The tales of both Shapeshifter and Skinwalker,
whether they're being stalked or being the stalkers—

Sofia and Sadie, so willing to do whatever it takes
to correct injustices and the king's mistakes.
So they came from the heavens to right the wrongs,
Shapeshifter and Skinwalker, oft told in songs.

The Ice Queen

Cold rain swirled and fell hard on that black and ominous night
as she entered the roadside inn resplendent in candlelight.
She was disguised in a shepherd's cloak to hide her chain mail
and looked around the low-ceilinged room to see every detail.

She moved slowly to a specific spot to choose a specific table.
She chose that vantage point for a reason for there she was able—
ever so determined to finish the deed once and for all—
to keep her eye on the door and her back to the wall.

The fire in the hearth warmed mutton and potato stew
as the serving boy placed in front of her a mug of their brew.
The inn was crowded and noisy, and at times tempers flared.
She knew they didn't have a clue and were so unprepared

for what would take place that night. When it was through,
in its aftermath, doom and destruction would be all they knew.
A minstrel took a place by the hearth and began to tune his harp.
The din in the room quieted as he was about to start.

He wiped his mouth with his sleeve after downing his beer.
She noticed a small diamond stud attached to his ear.
They listened to sweet music as he began to play
and heard his voice as he spoke up to say

the introduction of the ballad he was about to tell.
She sat back in her chair and listened as well.
She knew the outcome while sipping her ale.
The minstrel strummed his harp as he began his tale.

He sang a story of young love found and lost.
Heartbreak was ultimately the lover's cost.
Everyone was listening intently to the sad song,
but something seemed off. Something seemed wrong.

His fingers furiously thrummed the strings of his instrument
while his feet tapped keeping the rhythm and, in that instant,
he cast his glance at the audience and his expression became odd
because his neck was slowly turning and making his head nod.

His music and voice started to accelerate and race.
His eyes became large, and blood rushed to his face.
His actions became dismissive and, oh, so cavalier.
He was unhampered by restrictions. That was very clear.

The crowd drew back in horror at what they then saw
as horns grew out from his head. As he opened his jaw,
the room was silent as he hollered, "Is there no one here for me?"
They heard a wolf howl in the darkness the answer perhaps to be.

The wolf entered moving silently from the back of the inn
then sat on its haunches by the minstrel, directly beside him.
The woman in the shepherd's cloak knew the time was near.
The time of the reckoning was becoming so clear.

The minstrel stood up, and a flash of light came forth from his hands
as he shouted, "This is all for you, so everyone understands."
Hot fire he directed to ignite timbers in the ceiling and floor.
With hands in the air, patrons in the room screamed to implore,

begging mercy from the minstrel demon who had to settle a score.
The wolf leaped and snapped as they looked on in horror.
Patrons dashed under tables or anything to hide for cover
as they squealed in terror causing their bodies to tremble and shudder.

Minutes before, they were enjoying life from whence they came.
Burned, bitten, and injured for the nonce, they cried out in pain.
There was no one to confront the wolf and demon or to interfere
as the demon called "Laila, where are you? For I am here."

From the back of the room, a figure slowly rose from her chair.
The woman in the shepherd's cloak said, "I see you've finally come out of
your lair."
The man turned to face her while grinning as his wolf leaped at her neck,
but something caught it in midair as the woman threw a fleck

of icicle darts in its direction from her fingertips.
They froze the wolf from his tail all the way to his lips.
It turned to ice and fell to shatter on the floor.
The demon in his fury began to edge toward the door.

The fire he threw at her had no effect
as an invisible ice shield surrounded her to protect.
From under her cloak, she drew out a long sword of brilliant white.
Frost dashed along its edges up to its sharp point, it shone so bright.

Approaching the figure who drew back in alarm and dismay,
she quickly slashed frozen marks with her sword back and forth on her prey.
The demon minstrel screamed as his fire dissipated.
Then he turned blue, broke into pieces, and was all but obliterated.

She stood motionless for a moment, and then with a sigh,
lowered her long sword, for there was no one else to defy.
Silence in the room followed in the aftermath
as witness to what had just occurred and taken place and its wrath.

And then the realization, as far as witnesses could tell,
the demon had come there for her, and she had waited for him as well.
Hearing moaning and the cries of all who were in gloom,
she looked around at the scene in the smoke-filled room.

She knelt and tended the wounded and bandaged their injuries
while some gathered around waiting for her to explain mysteries.
Why had it happened and who was the horned demon at the hearth
and who was she, the one they witnessed, and what was she worth?

The mass carnage they had all just endured:
was it she or him who brought it to them and lured?
Some standing nearby stared at her as if at a ghost.
"Who is this woman?" was the question foremost.

As survivors huddled together, they waited. Before she spoke,
she stood tall before them and slowly unfastened her cloak
to an emblem of a white sword above a white glacier
and underneath her chain mail a white crown stitched to her blazer.

They all gaped in awe at it, those poor and unfortunate folk,
realizing the importance before them, and not a word they spoke,
for they knew the tale of the one who wore that marking was sacred.
'twas before them the Ice Queen herself, the one considered sainted.

"I am Laila," she said, "and you know why I am here,"
then continued in a voice angelic and with spirit to endear.
"The figures who appeared this night were two of the three,
and I will slay them all. That is my promise to thee."

The people kissed her hands and put their hands on her feet.
For her protection, their thanks they would continue to repeat,
but she knew in her heart and said silently under her breath,
"It won't be easy to defeat the three: doom, destruction, and death."

Doom was the one they named for the spirit wolf devil.
Destruction was the horned demon, the one of the next level,
while Death was the one still awaiting her arrival.
Defeating that one would test her survival.

So, two down and one to go,
the weather turned colder with the first signs of snow.
Seeking and searching but with nothing planned,
she wandered and wandered throughout the land

till a day when she saw a vagabond sitting off the side of the road,
his backpack removed from his shoulders to lighten his load.
He motioned her over to come sit by his campfire
and thought of what to say as to inquire,

"What are you doing by yourself, a woman on this road alone?
Don't you know it's dangerous, although death you can't postpone?
When it's your time, it's your time, or so they say."
He then looked up at the skies as they began to get dark and grey.

She didn't answer right away and thought something amiss
and knew at that moment not to be careless or remiss,
for her senses gave her hints not to dismiss,
or she might be facing her own abyss.

Her hand went to the handle, and it gripped her long sword.
The vagabond continued to talk, her silence apparently ignored.
But she saw he saw her hand move to her sword sheath,
and he looked into her eyes and with a smile of yellow teeth,

said, "Dear, are you afraid to be sitting here with me
just a lonely vagabond by the road, but, oh, so carefree?
Is there something about me that you foresee?
What do they say? Is it thirty or three?

"And if it were specifically three, what would that be?
Do the names all start with the letter D?"
Then the flames from the fire became hotter and hotter.
He waved his arms to form a circle of fire around her.

He fanned the flames, and they grew higher and higher.
Her ice-shield protection melted and turned into water.
When she tried to reach out with her sword, fire burned her arms.
With disdain, he shouted, "You can't touch me with your magic charms,

for I am Death, and tonight you're all mine.
Death waits for no one and takes when it's your time."
Her body rose in the air as fire burned her skin,
but she came down, forcing him to the ground with her shin.

Clutching him tightly, that one full of sin,
she shot ice bolts from her eyes to penetrate his skin.
Anguish was all she could see in his eyes,
all that there was under the night's grey skies.

Tales are told of it and the demon's demise.
Was that Death and the Ice Queen? Did both of them die?
Some say they saw the Ice Queen arise.
Whatever the case, in history she is lionized.

Some say she rests by the shoulder of the one above.
She's an everlasting symbol of empathy and love
for the deeds she accomplished while she was here.
She's one considered sainted, her spirit endeared.

The Keyhole

He cautiously ascended from the second-floor keep.
The stairs to the tower top above were narrow and steep.
He was not as young as he used to be,
but in the tower above he'd have his privacy.

He sat on the cold stone floor and at the ceiling he stared,
but his mind was elsewhere and he was scared
of what was happening inside those castle walls,
the nights interrupted by shouts and calls.

For the queen had gone mad or so the gossip said.
Some even suggested she'd be better off dead.
Keeping all and everything inside for forever, he swore.
He, the king, had locked her in with guards at her door

because of what he saw peeping through the keyhole—
nightmare visions inside that could steal your soul—
everything he saw inside and everything he saw there.
But I must warn you before proceeding to beware,

because we'll see what he sees behind the queen's door,
those he saw trapped there for evermore.
Thirteen visions, each related by two letters—
that is what he saw through the keyhole, his eyes meeting hers,

for looking back at him were the queen and the visions.
The door tightly locked was the only decision.
So, once again, the time to look had come,
and overwhelmed with temptation he would succumb.

Vision 1: A & B

He saw absurd aging alchemists mixing acids and arcane additives,
aware of their aura to always affect.
There in the background bawdy ballads were bellowed
by beefy bald bards in a distinct dialect.

Vision 2: C & D

He saw colorful cuckoos clinging to climbing clematis
and the queen in the middle wearing a crown of cactus
while demented dwarves with dangerous daggers
danced and dueled to further distract us.

Vision 3: E & F

He saw eels entwined each and everywhere
with their ebony eyes like embers, eerie and evil
followed by fearful fawns, their faces flawed.
They frowned at their forelegs, weakened and feeble.

Vision 4: G & H

He saw ghastly grinning grey and green ghosts
holding trays of gold grapes as if they were hosts
while hot-pink herons hung hats on hooks,
each one carrying bags with holes, their pocketbooks.

Vision 5: I & J

He saw indescribable idiots indiscriminately ironing
indigo images on felt
joined by jabbering jesters, their jaws pierced with jewels.
They juggled jugs of jellybeans to melt.

Vision 6: K & L

He saw a crimson Komodo dragon in a kooky kilt.
It blew kisses to a keyboard in its lap it kept
while little lizards leaped on lowlying limbs.
So long but so lost, with tears they wept.

Vision 7: M & N

He saw morose, mad, masked magenta mice
studiously making massive magic maps
while nervous nobles knelt nearby
in their Napierian, green, nylon nightcaps.

Vision 8: O & P

He saw old obese orange owls
obsessing over opaque orbs of oak
while they placed pink pythons in various pots,
with a pole and a poke.

Vision 9: Q & R

The queen had been so very quiet,
but with a start quickly queried with a quip,
"Who ruined my rare round ruby rose rug,
the one rimmed with gemstones? Because there's a rip!"

Vision 10: S & T

With a seedy scowl and the shrill sound of a shrew,
"Someone should swiftly sew it," suddenly shouted she.
Tailors immediately took to the task to tweak, tie, and tape,
asking for her forgiveness on their bended knee.

Vision 11: U & V

He saw utterly unhappy lepers, oh, so unloved,
sitting under eucalyptus trees colored in stripes.
Everywhere vexing venomous vipers slithered
while vaping battery powered vermillion pipes.

Vision 12: W & X

At the queen's feet, wizards wept and wailed,
for they were wearing the after effects—welts from a whip.
In an environment so xeric as if scraped with a xyster,
their hands held a xenium in a bag for the queen to unzip.

Vision 13: Y & Z

He saw young yellow yeomen yip and yawn,
their hands busily yarning bark from the trees of yew.
And lastly, zany zebras zooming and zig-zagging zealously
while they flew around everyone inside and above them, too.

Overwhelmed by those visions, the king fell back from the door,
screaming out, "Enough, enough. I can't take anymore."
Suddenly, three men burst into the room.
They then seized him. He experienced foredoom.

"I'm the king," he shouted. "It's not me. It's the queen.
This is not right, a mistake," he yelled, as he asked "Haven't you seen?"
They wrestled and tied him down and onto the floor.
He heard the lock click when they left and slammed the door.

Alas, he wasn't a king, for only he believed that.
He stared at the cushioned walls from where he sat.
He had lost his freedom and along with it his soul
from peeping at visions through the keyhole.

The Little Riddle Queen

Gather around for this story I will tell
of mystical creatures and a contest as well,
of a little girl with her hair all curled
who would become the ruler of a magical world.

The Beginning

So, picture the vision of a little girl skipping along a meandering forest path. It was very soft under her feet because spruce needles and moss covered the particular path. And along the way, although the woods were sometimes thick, she could see sunlight coming through the canopy. Beams of sun rays filtered through the forest trees and leaves.

But then her eyes widened in amazement as she glimpsed movement ahead in a small clearing. She approached cautiously and parted some brush with her hands and peered through. What she saw before her were creatures she had never seen, and they therefore looked strange.

One had the body of a man but legs of a deer.
He was playing a lute, his music a delight to the ear.
He was prancing about on his two hooves
ever so graceful with all his moves.
Beside him was another man with the head of a hawk.
He beat a drum softly in rhythm and seemed quite content.
What an odd pair, she thought.

But then the man who was part deer stopped what he was doing and looked in her direction. He saw her peering through the brush.
He called out to her . . .
"I see you there, but don't feel any fright,
You have nothing to fear. It will be alright.

Come closer now, for I will not bite.

Are you a wandering mythical wight?"

The little girl replied,

"I am not a wight. I'm a little girl."

She said it with a flourish and a little twirl.

As she emerged into the clearing and the light,

she tried to look brave with all her might.

"Aha," said the man with legs of a deer.

"What honor do we have that brings you here?"

He then said to her sarcastically, "A little girl alone in the forest, whatever could you be looking for? Oh, don't be secretive with me, for I know what you seek. You want to know about the competition, don't you?"

The little girl shook her head, confused, and asked, "Competition?"

"Yes, yes, yes . . . competition, competition. You're here because you want my riddle."

It didn't make any sense to her at all, so she said,

"Please sir can you please explain?

Please tell it to me and make it plain."

To answer, he replied,

"Well, well, well, let me see.

Have you not heard of the decree?

"Well, I'll spell it out for you, little girl. It is called by the council of four, Owl, Lion, Wolf, and Elephant. They determine who will be chosen queen of the land.

"And why these four, you may ask? Why, for what each of them has to offer—Owl for her wisdom, Lion for strength, Wolf for its cunning, and Elephant for his memory. If someone can answer the riddle, each of them will ask, they will award the crown to that person.

"Unfortunately, the crown is vacant at present, thus the competition.

"You see?

"So don't beat around the bush. You want a hint of the riddles, don't you? 'tis said that for each special one you meet along this forest path, they'll give you a riddle, if so inclined. That way, you can mull it around and try to figure out the answers if you can."

He then muttered under his breath to the man with a head of a hawk, "Ha, that will never happen."

"So, if you think you're up to the task," he said to the girl, "I give you your first riddle.

"On a clear day and upon the sea,
if you look up or down, what do you see?
When you are depressed or melancholy and on your knees,
what one word describes all of these?

"As I said, good luck with that. You may be on your way now. Follow the path, and around the bend, you may be lucky enough to find a special wren with a tulip on its head and wings of pure gold.

"That is how you will know it is the one."

The Wren

So off went the little girl a bit amused by the story she had been told. Nonetheless, she was young and naturally curious to see what might happen next and where the path would ultimately lead her. On her way, she thought about the riddle without much concentration because she had to keep her eyes keenly attuned to her surroundings in order to find the wren.

Because wrens are small, you know.

Around the bend, she began to hear a quiet chirp repeating over and over the same phrase. "Welcome, welcome little girl, you have found the one you are looking for." As the chirping grew louder, she looked up and saw a wren perched on a tree limb with its beautiful golden wings sparkling in the light of the day. Atop its head was a plume made of fine tulips.

The girl said,
"I believe you are the one I am to see."
The wren replied,
"Yes, yes, yes, indeed
Come over here to sit and talk with me,
and I will make us both some tea."

Now, I know that sounds odd, and I can't explain how the wren could make tea nor have the cups and saucers and anything else needed. Presently, though, it did become clear as they both partook of what children sometimes do. Together, they had an imaginary tea party. So as the little girl pretended to hold a cup and sip her tea, the wren with the tulip plume began to speak.

"So, I know why you're here and what you want from me. Listen closely to what I say as I recite to you the second riddle. I don't want you to forget anything, because you seem to be such a sweet little girl. And I would love to sit here and chat, but I know you're in a rush, so here goes:

"It could be a prize awarded to the winner of a race,
or something used to claim land if that was the case
or then again used when placing a wager,
if a gambler would take that risk and danger.
What one word describes all of those?"

The little girl put down her imaginary cup and said to the wren, "Thank you for the tea and the riddle you have told. Where now do I go?"

"Keep walking down till you reach the river. Then follow the path along the banks until you see the Elf. He will have further instructions for you. Good luck to you little girl."

And off the wren flew.

The Elf

An elf, thought the girl.

That might be nice as she thought of winter holiday stories. Perhaps she would find him under a Christmas tree, one like a spruce or evergreen. She gaily sauntered on down to the riverbed and followed the path along the riverbanks as she had been told. But nowhere could she find that elf. She searched high and low under the brush and the trees nearby. But with no luck, she became weary so lay down on a grassy spot by the water to rest.

Who should appear from out the woods but the elf! She knew why she couldn't find him. He had blended in well with his surroundings as all the clothes he wore were of forest greens, and he even had green smudged on his face.

He was no ordinary elf. His ears were long and pointed, but he was tall and lithe, his features pale and fair and perfect. He appeared to be a hunter with his bow and arrows slung over his shoulder. It was hard to tell how old he was because it is said elves have magical powers not to age or to age very slowly.

So, of course, she was taken aback at the sight, but he approached her calmly and had a big grin on his face.

He said, "You must be the little girl who, I'm told, is on a special journey. I've found you."

She looked at him and replied, "I thought I was supposed to find you."

He laughed heartily and said, "No matter. The outcome is the same."

He sat down beside her and stretched his legs before removing the bow and arrows and placing them by his side. Then he began to talk.

"There are not many who would do this quest," he said.

"You must be a very brave little girl. I can see that you are very special, so I'll give up my riddle to you to take as you will. So here it is:

"Something its working suddenly ceases

or damage results in multiple pieces

or something contrary to an agreement or rule

by someone smart or considered a fool—

what one word describes all of those?

"I wish you well on your journey little girl," he added. "Be safe, and I bid you farewell."

As he rose up, the girl quickly said, "Thank you, Sir Elf, for spending this time with me, for sharing your riddle and your company. But there is one more thing I need to know. Where is it from here should I go?"

"Follow the river from here to a place where it is narrower. You will find at that spot a tree that has fallen, and you can walk across, for you must cross the river and up over that hill to seek the last one you need, the woman called the Bell Lady. All four riddles you need before approaching the council."

And then he added with a smile, "If that is your intention."

She nodded.

The Bell Lady

She walked up and over the hill and soon heard the sound of tinkling bells. Curious, she headed in that direction. She saw an old woman sitting in a soft cushioned chair, its fabric composed of images of multicolored bells. To the little girl, she appeared to be at least a hundred years old as she hunched over holding onto a crooked cane.

The old lady had long earrings made of tiny bells tied together in a strand. She had bells on her belt buckle and bells tied on her shoes. On her wrists, she wore bell bracelets and even bells attached to her cane. Obviously, any slight movement she made caused the bells to all jingle and jangle.

"Hello, dear," the old woman said.

"You must be the Bell Lady," replied the little girl.

"I am. What can I do for you?"

"I've been told you have a riddle for me."

"Is that so? Well, you know people say a lot of things about me, and I never cared for busybodies and such. And anyway, as you can see, I am very old, and if I had had a riddle, I don't seem to remember it."

"Well, I hope you can recall, because it is the final one I need so I can go to the competition."

"Well, that does sound important. so let me think about this for a minute."

The old woman closed her eyes as the little girl watched her intently. Then she noticed the woman looked like she was falling asleep. And sure enough, she soon heard the sound of a low snore. She reached over to touch the old lady's arm gently with her fingers.

"What? Who are you? What do you want?" the old lady asked, startled.

The little girl replied, "You were trying to remember the riddle."

"My, my, you're a persistent little one. But I must say it is a quality that sometimes comes in handy. Okay, let's see. I do know that I write a lot of things down, so perhaps that's what I did. Come with me."

She got up from the chair with effort, the little girl holding her arm for support, and they made their way to an opening carved out in the trunk of a large tree. As they passed through the opening, the little girl saw a large chest of drawers against one side of the interior wall. The chest consisted of twenty-six drawers, each with a letter of the alphabet inscribed on it.

"Oh, I need my glasses," said the old lady. "I can't see anything without them. Now where did I put them? Perhaps here?" The old lady moved to the chest and opened the drawer marked with a large G. Sure enough, the glasses were inside, and she put them on.

"Well," said the old lady. "That's much better. So as to this riddle you speak of, let me see," she said, her fingers rubbing her chin. She pulled out the drawer marked R, rifled through the papers inside, and then pulled out a card.

"Ah, yes, here it is! I will read this to you, sweet child:
"Something that lacks ornament of any kind,
or, if one speaks obvious and clear of mind.
Or it could be lacking ugliness or beauty—this I tease—
what one word describes all of these?"

And as the old lady gave the young girl the card, the old woman said, "I have something else for you," and reached up to a shelf hanging on the wall and picked up a small silver bell.

"Take this as my gift to you. Keep it in your pocket for good luck."

The little girl said, "Thank you so much. You are so kind. I will always treasure this little silver bell! And I don't want to be a further nuisance, but can you tell me where I will find the Great Hall, as that is where I'm told the competition takes place."

The Bell Lady replied, "You're almost there. If you look down into the valley below you will see it. Remember it starts at six. Don't be late! Goodbye, little girl" and she went back inside the hollowed-out tree trunk.

Reflections

Sure enough, as the little girl looked down from the hill, there in the middle of the valley stood a large gleaming building, the Great Hall, just as the Bell Lady had described.

Since it was still early, the little girl sat down and thought about the most extraordinary day. The man who was part deer was gruff and not that nice, but he had told her all about the competition and had given her the riddle. The wren had been so sweet, and she genuinely enjoyed her company and hoped to see her again. The elf was worldly, knowledgeable, and quite friendly and, after all, he had found her. The old Bell Lady reminded her of her own grandmother in some ways. *You can learn a lot from old people, as they have so many life experiences to share—if they can remember,* she thought with a giggle. And the Bell Lady gave her a gift for good luck, just like grandmas do.

She thought, *Just because you're regarded as being one so young doesn't mean you don't know what's going on. Isn't this just like anyone you meet in your life? Some nice, some not so, but those moments shared together each have something to offer in their own unique way.* With no judgment, she loved them all for what they were, and isn't that how it should be?

She thought about the riddles and mulled it about just like the man who was part deer said she would. She attempted to find the words that described each verse. She had some ideas but wasn't completely sure, but she was determined to do what she always did. She would do her best. So she picked herself up and hiked down the trail leading to the valley.

The Competition

She reached the valley floor and headed toward the Great Hall. Soon the roads and surroundings became densely packed with an assortment of all types of creatures and unusual beings who had come from everywhere in the land—from east, west, north, and south, all traveling to the Great Hall to witness the remarkable event.

There were large ogres, and the ground shook when they walked by. There were minotaurs and trolls, and she even saw a few white unicorns mingling in the crowds. There were beings dressed in elaborate robes while others wrapped themselves in fine silks. There were elves and animals of all different sorts, and there were fairies who floated in the air above the throngs. She saw all that and much, much more.

As she entered the hall, there was much gaiety. Acrobats did tricks, and musicians played their instruments. Waiting with anticipation, all those who had come gathered inside. A line of storks on each side of the hallway held trumpets to their lips. Dressed in short red blazers with gold buttons, each wore a hat the shape that Napoleon used to wear.

The trumpets blared as she entered the hall. Then the crowds parted slowly to let the little girl through.

As she walked, she looked up into the balconies above and saw there the man who was part deer, the wren, and the elf looking down and waving at her. And just as the great doors were closing behind her, in hobbled the Bell Lady to give her a wink and then take a seat just inside.

The little girl walked forward and stood alone in front of a high wooden dais with the Council of Four, Owl, Lion, Wolf, and Elephant seated atop.

Owl struck his gavel loudly four times on a wooden box to bring all those in attendance to silence and indicate the opening of the proceedings.

Owl addressed the little girl. "It has come to our attention," said Owl, "that you are here for the competition. Be aware that this is a very solemn event and a very, very, very important and special, special day. As you are the only one, we will proceed.

"But before we start, I am required to read the official decree." And he brought forth a scroll that had been tucked under his wing and started to unroll it until its length reached to the floor. "By order of this royal document it is hereby stated," he read, then his eyes began to scan and skip through the words. He continued with, ". . . something about historical facts, mentions of rules, and this and that, and so on and so on and so forth."

He rolled the scroll back up, tucked it under his wing, and announced, "Now that we are done with the formalities, let us begin!"

Trumpets blared.

To the little girl he said, "Understand that you will be asked a riddle, one from each of the council members." To the gathered crowds, he said, "We will listen to her answers and make our determination."

Owl peered over his spectacles as he looked down at her. "Here is my riddle.

> "On a clear day and upon the sea,
> if you look up or down what do you see?
> When you are depressed or melancholy and on your knees,
> what one word describes all of these?"

There was a hush in the Great Hall as the little girl spoke.

"If it is a clear day and I look up at the sky, it is blue. If I'm on the sea and look down into the water, it is also blue. And sometimes when I'm sad, my mother says I'm feeling blue.

So, in answer to your riddle, my answer is blue."

"Hmmmm," said Owl and, turning to Lion beside him, said, "Lion, you may proceed."

Lion stuck out his chest and in a booming voice said, "Here is my riddle:

> "It could be a prize awarded to the winner of a race,
> or something used to claim land if that was the case,
> or then again used when placing a wager,
> if a gambler would take that risk and danger,
> what one word describes all of these?"

The little girl replied, "If the race was a horse race, the one who crosses the finish line first takes the stake as in the Belmont or Preakness."

There was a murmur in the crowd. They had never heard of the Belmont or Preakness.

Owl banged his gavel. "Quiet in the hall!"

The little girl resumed, "Regarding land? I suppose if you wanted a plot of land, you could mark your boundary with a stake. Or to claim property you could use the word stake, sort of like to stake your claim.

"As for gambling I don't know much about that. But what they are considering for a bet I've heard can be referred to as a stake.

"So, considering all that, I would say in answer to your riddle, my answer is stake."

Wolf bent forward, and his beady eyes focused intently on the little girl before him.

"Here is my riddle:

"Its workings suddenly cease or damage results

in multiple pieces or something contrary

to an agreement or rule

by someone smart or considered a fool.

What one word describes all of these?"

The little girl knew the cunning of Wolf and was careful in her response. She felt there might be a trick to his riddle. And just in case, with her hand in her pocket, she rubbed the little silver bell with her fingers for good luck as the Bell Lady had told her.

"Well, if it's something that no longer works, you could say its broken. As for damage you might say it was broken into many pieces. If a fool, I think, it means a law could be broken. If smart and negotiating a more favorable agreement, the old one would be broken. So, in answer to your riddle, my answer is broken."

It was Elephant's turn. His trunk lay across the table where they sat on the dais and over the other side. It was said he could remember all the history of those lands, due to the fact that elephants have great memories.

"Here is my riddle:

"Something that lacks ornament of any kind or,

if one speaks obvious and clear of mind or

it could be lacking ugliness or beauty.

This I tease. What one word describes all of these."

The little girl thought for a moment, then said, "With no decoration at all it would be considered plain. If one were to speak to me as you say, I would say that is speaking it plain. And for your third proposition, I would say it would have to be in between, therefore plain. So, in response to your riddle, my answer is plain."

There was complete silence in the hall as the Council of Four, Owl, Lion, Wolf, and Elephant huddled together to confer. They completed their deliberations and made a decision. They all four came down from the dais and stood in front of the little girl. Before making their announcement, they held in front of them a large, ornate pillow with golden tassels. In one trunk or wing or paw, each council member held one corner of the pillow. On the pillow rested a diamond tiara bejeweled with other precious gems.

Council President Owl addressed the little girl in a voice that carried throughout the Great Hall so all the assembled crowd could hear.

"Come forward, little girl. Your answers were correct. This honorary title is granted, for you have passed our test. We hereby declare you queen of our land. All creatures, people, half people, and any other unusual beings of every other sort and so on and so on will be your loving subjects forevermore."

And with that proclamation. he placed on her head the diamond tiara with other precious gems.

The storks blew their trumpets, and everyone jumped up and down, shouting in glee. The musicians played merry music, and many in the crowd danced with joy. They hugged each other.

Some even approached the little girl to kiss her hand and tell her how happy they were that she was their queen. They said they were happy and proud because their ruler was so smart. The little girl felt overwhelmed at all the delight and revelry. She also felt a little faint at all the commotion.

She began to feel dizzy . . . so dizzy.

The Conclusion

She was in her bed. She looked around. Yes, she felt certain it was her bedroom. She was back home again?

She looked out her window as the sun rose in the morning. She jumped out of bed and couldn't wait to tell her mother all about her adventure and all about the man who was part deer, the wren, the elf, Bell Lady, Owl, Lion, Wolf, and Elephant and how she had won the crown. For she had been crowned queen of a very magical land.

She talked to her mother all day long about what she had seen and done.

That evening at bedtime, she looked around her room for something missing that was important to her. She searched everywhere but had no luck. So, she climbed into her bed and tucked her hands under her pillow.

She felt an object.

Tossing the pillow aside, she found a little silver bell, its origin not of this world.

Lorelei

The young man sought adventure as he walked along the docks.
He stopped in front of a merchant ship, the one they called the *Blue Fox*.
The first mate looked him over and agreed to hire him on,
for he was strong and healthy, and they could certainly use his brawn.

He walked up on the gangplank to see sailors hoisting sails
and pulling ropes along the deck, they tugged from the ship deck rails
cargo raised in nets from the pier to the ship above.
Then they lowered crates into the hold with a steady push and shove.

The crew swabbed down the decks with water from their pails,
and then pulled up the heavy anchor and prepared to set the sails.
As he gazed out over the harbor and the ship began to move,
the young man reflected on the choice he made, for his worth he was to prove.

As the ship moved to deeper waters with the land slowly left behind,
he followed the first mate's orders for whatever he was told or assigned.
The work was hard and strenuous, but he loved being on the sea—
the experience of a lifetime he felt. It was where he wanted to be.

He had an evening meal of salted meat and
hard biscuits washed down with ales.
The crew sat together at night to tell some of their lofty sea tales.
The young man listened to all those stories so embellished and overdone—
Of pirates and huge sea monsters or hidden treasures to be
found by someone.

He enjoyed being in their company, all those rough and rowdy men.
They were like a band of brothers till they saw their loved ones again.
They lived the hard life on the seas, but when land appeared to be near,
they'd clap each other on the back and with their voices they would cheer.

The young man stood and watched from the starboard to see the setting sun,
and as darkness filled the sky above, the stars slowly appeared one by one.
He went down to his sleeping quarters, his hammock slung between the beams.
And there he slept a quite sound sleep,
his thoughts wrapped up in pleasant dreams.

But in the middle of the night, he awoke to shouts from the upper deck,
alarm sounding in their voices. So he went up the stairs to check.
The lookout up in the crow's nest yelled, "Black clouds I see approach."
Then he hurriedly scrambled down the ropes as the storm began to encroach.

The quartermaster screamed aloud, calling all hands up to the deck.
The ship was ever so tilting, leaning closer to the water's depths.
But it was hard to hear the captain's orders as the wind did loudly howl.
The sailors were scared and anxious, and the quartermaster showed a scowl.

He shouted, "Button down the hatches, boys, and unfurl the sails to wrap,
before the stormy winds get worse, and cause the masts to snap."
They gathered their ropes together to tie all the loose things down.
They pulled their knots with all their might to make sure
all was securely bound.

Waves washed over the deck and caused the sailors to slip and slide,
some of them so overcome with fear as they just held on and cried.
Unlucky crewmates were tossed overboard when waves crashed down on them.
Others yelled out their prayers to God above to please intervene and stem

the awful, thunderous storm that appeared with no warning to prepare—
with winds of sea mist and waves of salt water swirling around in the air.
The ship began to creak and groan as waves continued to pound.
The sailors' eyes revealed them scared and shocked
watching their ship mates drown.

The ballast they placed in the hold shifted position with a start,
and then the wood timbers that supported the bow split and tore apart.
The ship was slowly sinking, and as it rolled onto its side,
into the waters of the chilly deep sea, the ship *Blue Fox* did slide.

Any who survived that tragedy gasped deeply for breaths of air
as waves tossed and turned them all about, freezing them with despair.
The young man grabbed the side of a raft, and someone there hauled him on.
Around them they heard men calling for help,
then silence as others were gone.

They were swept away in the darkness on waves that crested and fell.
The young man and one other clinging to the timber of the raft on each swell.
Wind and rolling waves continued as
the storm pushed them through the night.
When it finally grew quiet and subsided, they were the only two in sight.

They were wet and soaked and exhausted by the time of early dawn.
Each realized at that moment in nature's wrath each was just a pawn.
The one who had pulled him onto the raft, the one who saved him from the sea
was the experienced sailor he had first met when hired,
the First Mate Jackson Ree.

Jackson said, "We're in a pickle here, boy,
but there's not much that we can do—
just hope and pray we see a passing ship or
perhaps a bit of land in our view."

And every day thereafter, the sun rose and was high and hot.
With lack of food and clean water,
their minds began to twist their thought.
They could only sit and bake in the heat as they drifted on endlessly
so hopelessly helpless to the ocean's currents upon the endless sea.

Their faces burnt, their lips were cracked, and
their mouths were, oh, so dry.
First Mate Jackson Ree often stared with a look that signified,
for he knew the outcome was becoming clear and that it would verify
the ending of his life on the seas. To the seas he would bid goodbye.

Then Jackson suddenly stood up and with a teeter and a totter—
tipped right off the side of the raft with a splat into the water.
The young man jumped up quickly and, peering over the side,
saw Jacksons body disappear into the depths as it took its downward ride.

So then the young man floated alone, and what would become of him?
His situation was deteriorating, and everything was becoming grim.
On it went, and it seemed forever, one day just becoming the next.
What was real and what was not? He hallucinated due to the effects.

Then all of a sudden, he heard the sound of a splash and
turned his head to see
a fish tail flapping the water. What could the strange sight be?
Then the head of a beautiful woman appeared.
She had long flowing golden hair.
Was she the mythical creature they talk about, the one they say is so rare?

She swam up to sit beside him, that one-half human, one-half fish.
"I want you to be my merman—," she said as her tail flapped with a swish.
"—to be my husband under the sea in a water world full of bliss."
She stated it quite clearly and then sealed it with a kiss.

She told him her name was Lorelei, a daughter of the king and queen
of the merfolk under the waters in the underworld of blue and green.
And then she told him truly for him to understand
that his situation was very dire, but she had an alternative plan.

"There's no one else here to find you. That much you know is true,
and if you stay here any longer, your human life will be through.
So come with me, and I promise an adventure for just us two,
for isn't that what you first wanted when you set sail upon the blue?"

She dove into the water, and he dove in right behind,
swimming deeper and much farther to see what he would find.
He knew it was the right decision to leave the world of mankind.
He was on another adventure, the mermaid and himself entwined—

holding each other's hands while swimming brought him peace of mind.
He would treasure those moments together for however long the time.
She brought him to her underworld and introduced him to all:
octopus, squid, and various fish, all the creatures both big and small.

Passing by stingrays and seahorses as they made their way to her home,
he saw the many spines of sea urchins and ahead a geodesic dome.
He marveled at its beauty, for it was carved from such colorful coral.
In arrangements of colors and textures, it appeared to be almost floral.

All the merfolk they were waiting, King Merman and Queen Mermaid, too,
to witness the wonderful occasion in their underworld of blue,
the marriage under the beautiful dome.
And when the ceremony was through,
he became a merman and bid his previous life adieu.

A Tale from Timbuktu

The man was dark skinned, his face marked with tattoo,
and around his head was wrapped a silk turban of blue.
The wind whipped the dunes, and the sand in the air blew.
He sat atop his camel to see the city finally come into view,
the legendary city of Timbuktu.

For so long they had traveled the Sahara Desert, those two,
and felt relief as the skies cleared the nearer they drew
to the city named after the Tuareg woman Boctoo—
finally home at last to the city he grew up in, loved, and knew,
the legendary city of Timbuktu.

Situated north of the River Niger where dusty roads appear through,
considered by all a major trade route of the Sahara, it was true,
its beige walls and beige mosque towers in slight variations of hue—
the city well known for gold, salt, and knowledge, too—
the legendary city of Timbuktu.

Islam influenced structures as their domed mosques grew.
Scholars busily working as scribes their writings they did do.
Accumulating manuscripts and books for the city was their due,
for the place considered a great center of learning in many a view,
the legendary city of Timbuktu.

That was how it was that day when the man from the desert arrived.
Crossing the Sahara by camel with little food or drink,
he had barely survived.

Through the city gates, he entered enraptured and mesmerized
by and from vivid memories returning to him, and he realized,
he was back, back in the legendary city of Timbuktu.

He tied his camel to a post and walked through narrow dusty streets.
He listened to the banging of drums and their rhythmic drumbeats
announcing the presence of Arab and African traders who came
trading the salt they brought in return for gold, sums valued the same.

He passed by all the mud buildings in shapes like cones.
Mixing mud clay and reeds was how they built their homes.
He walked till he came to the bronze doors of the Dogon priest.
It was the home of the holy one and a sanctuary of peace.

Entering in on colored tiles cool on his bare feet
and passing one room lined from floor to ceiling so neat
with more books than he had ever seen, a sign of the elite.
A servant welcomed him into a room and presented a seat.

Among fine carpets and large pillows piled on the floor,
the servant brought a pitcher and glass for sweet tea to pour,
then asked him, "Is there anything else you might want for?"
"No, I am only here for trusted advisement with my mentor."

The master would join him soon, he was told, so he took a seat.
He buried his tattooed face in his hands and felt so incomplete,
for news that reached him in the desert had been bittersweet,
and he wanted to hear it from the priest, who would be discreet.

The woman he had truly loved had passed away,
so he spent years thereafter in the desert adrift and astray,
full of sorrow and distress and dismay.
But so many years later, here he lay

among the fine carpets and large pillows of blue,
to speak to the priest to find out if it was untrue or true.
Would it be a new beginning or a sad adieu
back in the legendary city of Timbuktu?

The priest bowed his head as he entered the room
and said to the man, "You're the one from the desert, I presume."
Then, recognizing his face, said "Ayad, how long has it been?"
Ayad replied, "It's been so long, teacher. Where do I begin?"

Ayad then told his story of his many years away.
He had felt his life over, so he began to stray.
He had been with a caravan when he heard the news
that his true love had died, so what did he choose?

To wander the desert from place to place,
never again to feel her warm embrace,
so he had never returned back to city he knew,
the legendary city of Timbuktu.

Ayad said, "The reason I come to you, holy one, now,
is for your interpretation of a strange vision that touched me somehow.
One night in the desert, the image of a young girl and a moonbeam
as I slept came from above and crept into my dream,

telling me the young girl I viewed was really my daughter
and to follow the moonbeam back to her, as she thought I forgot her.
I hadn't seen my wife before she passed for probably a year
due to the salt caravans I traveled with to the coasts for the emir.

"I followed the light from the moonbeam its request to pursue,
and the moonbeam led me all the way back here to Timbuktu.
Tell me, master, do I really have a child that I never knew?
Please tell me what you know and whether it's true."

The Master placed a hand on Ayad's shoulder and said,
"There is much for you to think about with such thoughts in your head.
I do know your wife was showing shortly after you left,
but if a child was born, I don't know before her death.

"But, strangely, I do know a girl called Khaira with a similar tale,
which she told me one night in very great detail,
a fantastic story, I thought, which I didn't believe,
until what you just described and how they may interweave.

"I found her on the street alone and glum.
No one seemed to know her or where she'd come from.
I took her in to protect her and taught her the ways
and traditions of Mali and of the god we praise."

The master called for the servant to bring Kaira so she could tell
the story she had told before, perhaps to foretell
a connection between her and Ayad. Had it occurred,
a magic bond between father and daughter? Had it endured?

In walked a girl with a tray of couscous, honey, and bread.
From her ears hung gold earrings wrapped with bright red thread.
She had many tattoos on her lips and chin,
her presence exuding a mysterious aura within.

The holy one beckoned her in and told her to sit
and to tell the man with him her story—to please re-tell it.
She sat down cross-legged on the carpets and pillows to state
her story to the master and stranger, as that was her fate.

She said,
"I went in search into the desert to find the viper of fame,
the one with seven heads and all-knowing, or so people claim.
I went willingly to the viper that has seven heads,
one no other goes close to nor near to tread.

"I came upon its rock dwelling and heard its hiss,
but I knew it was the only one who could give me this,
the answer I needed, so a promise to it I made.
Each of its heads I would kiss, and I was not afraid.

"The viper thought it a fair deal and, for the trade,
said, 'What is your question child? How can I aid?'
I told it, 'My father has been missing for over a decade,
and I need to find him. For that I have prayed.'

"I asked the viper who is it I should seek.
All fourteen eyes blinked before it would speak,
'Seek the wanderer who continually circles the earth,
but to reach that one, you will need these seeds of birth.'

"Pointing to the night sky, it said, 'That is where you must go—
to the full yellow moon above, for the answer he will know.'
I planted my seed from the viper, and it began to grow,
the vines crawling and twisting higher into the sky and so

"I climbed the vine ladder going higher and higher
till I saw his full face with my concern to inquire.
I made my request to the Man in the Moon."
He replied, 'I'll shed my light on every sand dune.

"'I will find your father and send down a moonbeam
along with the image of your face for him in a dream.
My message for him will be to follow the path,
and if he follows it truly awaiting its aftermath,
moonbeam light will lead him all the way back to you,
back to the legendary city of Timbuktu.'"

As she finished her story, Khaira looked at Ayad.
He stared at her saying, "I've been blessed by God."
His daughter had reached out to the powers that be,
and they realized at that moment the guarantee

that they had found each other, those special two,
father and daughter together at last in Timbuktu.
She had never given up hope and had been so brave.
To her search for her father, her whole heart she gave

along with her prayers and the Man in the Moon, too,
and the kisses she gave the all-knowing viper, who
had all helped her to find her father, she knew,
joyfully in the legendary city of Timbuktu.

In the Garden Maze

I emptied my mind with a flitter and flutter,
no words in my subconscious to think or utter.
I focused all of my thoughts, not making a stir,
hoping my night trance would soon reoccur.

Then it appeared with its visions to bring,
but I couldn't make sense of it nor of anything,
for whether I looked lengthwise or sideways,
I found myself in a deep garden maze.

Staring all around and at all of its edges,
I stood upon a pebbled path in a labyrinth of hedges.
Never before had I ever been brought there,
and as I listened closely, I became aware

of a melodious chant like monks would sing.
So peaceful it was, a sweet-sounding thing.
I began to walk, turning this way and that.
Then ahead I observed a calico cat

keeping distance from me but always looking back
to see if I followed to pursue its track
till it finally led me to a small open space
with a fountain in the middle—such a lovely place.

The cat jumped on the water basin, and down at its feet
was an ebony box, its appearance discreet.
The cat looked at me and then at the box.
There was a key on the lid to open the locks.

The top had an image, a white dragon painted.
The box looked ageless and so untainted,
I approached and knelt down, unlocking the lid
anxious to see inside, to see what it hid.

Its interior was of blue velvet with nothing inside.
The cat then moved closer with this to confide,
"My little lady, now, does nothing but cry,
for her brother hid the contents," it said that with a sigh.

"She's hiding in the garden and can't be consoled.
All she has left of it is a board to hold."
So I rose up then, holding the box in my hand,
asking "What do I look for? Help me understand."

The calico cat replied with only these words,
"You'll know when you see them, so say the birds."
So I offered my help to do what I could,
not knowing what I shouldn't do nor what I should.

I glanced all around me and then at different places,
checking all thoroughly throughout all of the spaces.
I walked many paths throughout the windy maze,
the cat trailing behind me as if in a daze.

Then to my astonishment, I began to see traces,
for peering back at me were little lost faces
poking out from the hedges. Their eyes showed through,
watching me closely to see what I would do.

Some were very clear, but some were a blur—
four miniature kings and queens, two each there were
like little, tiny beings but colorful ones,
and holding their hands were little black-clad nuns.

The kings and queens all wore sparkling crowns,
but on their faces, they only showed frowns.
And as they stepped forward parting the bush,
others then followed, perhaps by a push.

And more little people then began to emerge.
As they grouped together and began to converge,
ladies appeared in long dresses with lace all around.
They gently fanned their faces to help them cool down.

They wore pointed hats with flowing silk ribbons.
Their faces were powdered on those royal women,
sixteen in all, a distinct eight and eight
with half in silver and half in gold plate.

Bearded alchemists emerged wearing dark robes,
hovering stars above each, in their hands crystal globes.
Serious and studious they looked standing so erect
as their globes all pulsated with special effect.

Then, like armored toy riders or an order of chivalry,
came four knights on glass horses. Their banners they carried.
Two had silver flags and two had gold.
Each had stern faces, those nobles so bold.

Then from the hedges, four catapults appeared
pulled by men-at-arms, their faces smeared
with sweat and dirt as they struggled with might
due to tugging the ropes—it was their plight.

Then above them all, around and around it went.
A white dragon circled to guard with all its intent,
and like a butterfly does, gently beating its wings,
it then hovered above the two stately kings.

They all slowly walked out and stood at my feet.
They looked up at me wistfully as if waiting to greet.
Then a bard with a harp pushed his way to the front,
asking "What are you looking for, sir, on your hunt?"

I was taken aback and surprised: a little bard that talks?
I replied, "I'm looking for whatever belongs in this box."
The bard turned to the others and shouted, "He found it!"
Then to me he said, "Sir, if you will so permit,

"I will explain what happened. And just to be clear,
all we want is to get it back to the one we hold dear.
The little boy scattered us, and then he fled,
but all of us belong in the box!" is what the bard said.

"Take us back to whom we belong," he pled,
"—the one who loves us, the little child in red."
I opened the box lid, and in they all climbed.
Each group took its turn as if assigned,

the kings and queens first, as deemed their status,
then the fine ladies laid in a pattern of lattice.
The serious alchemists climbed in, too,
while the knights and their horses waited in queue.

Men at arms with their catapults—their turn came due.
In hopped the bard, blowing a kiss saying, "Thank you."
And lastly, into the box the dragon flew.
A happy reunion waited in store. That they all knew.

And jumping for joy was the calico cat,
saying, "I'll lead the way to where she's at."
It led me along paths till we reached the end,
and then I saw her, a child dressed in red around the bend.

She looked startled to see me till the cat said, "He's a friend."
Her eyes stared at the box. She tried to comprehend.
I turned the key as she uttered a gasp.
I opened the lid, unfastening the clasp.

Everyone inside waved and shouted to her,
"Back to where we belong, thanks to the good sir."
The little girl hugged her cat and then, looking at me,
said, "You've brought joy back to my life, as it should be.

"You've returned all the pieces for my wizard's chess game.
Each one is enchanted to move when I call their name."
She placed her board on the ground, and the players stood in line,
all the characters in place and looking, oh, so fine.

I said my goodbyes then, knowing the time had come.
I closed my eyes to return to where I'd come from,
stories to remember and adventures to be
in my mind's eye to enjoy. It brings them to me.

The Misgivings

She turned her head ever so slowly, and then she looked away,
for there was really nothing more either of us could say,
both knowing the fact was sadly true, that the end was drawing nigh
and both resigned to that outcome. And then I heard her cry.

She turned back to look at me, and her question was simply, "Why?"
But there was nothing I could say nor do to soothe nor justify,
for it was I whose actions had brought us here
to this woeful damp cold cell.
The hanging noose awaited us
when twelve chimes rang from the bell.

What led to this cruel ending for us? Isn't that what you want to know?
Sit back and listen to the tale, which began in a winter of wind and snow.
Most of the folk stayed in their homes as snow continued to fall.
Clouds hung low and gusting with wind, bringing in a wintry squall.

Autumn had ended early that year, and all the days were grey
as we prepared the horses to harness up and strap them to our sleigh.
My wife and child were bundled tight with furs of animal hides.
I checked the runners for any ice to make sure our movement would glide

smoothly across the snowy paths, for many more miles ahead we had.
As we left the village inn that day and the weather getting bad,
we began our trek back home again, anxious while there was still light,
planning to reach our village before the coming darkness of night.

The horses pulled us quickly along through lowlands and into the woods.
We tried to keep the wild winds at bay with our fur garments and hoods.
Suddenly I pulled back hard on the reins as we came upon a ghastly sight,
for the scene that appeared in front of us chilled us all with fear and fright.

Frozen bodies covered the road, and their sleighs were overturned,
and there by the side, it did appear, their belongings had been burned.
My wife was so appalled by the sight that she shielded our small child's eyes
as I checked all of the icy covered ones but found none I could recognize.

I realized, looking at some of them, they wore garments nobles would wear.
One was a young woman with opened eyes staring a deathly stare.
I noticed the wounds appeared to be caused by dagger or short sword,
and I thought the two oldest unlucky ones could be a lady and a lord.

Just then, I saw some movement behind one of the larger trees.
A pale thin figure on the ground urgently reached out and said, "Please."
He was dressed in diamond-patterned clothes that clung to him with frost.
"Please save me and take me with you," he pleaded. "I'll pay whatever cost."

I lifted him up and carried him to our sleigh and covered him with furs.
He was shivering so and mumbling, but I couldn't make out his words.
I climbed back into the sleigh to move cautiously and more aware,
that danger might lurk close by. We proceeded with utmost care.

But as the sleigh moved swiftly on, a remembrance came to mind,
of a dream I had had not that long ago—could it have been well timed?
I mentioned the vision to my wife, but she said she did not recall,
so once again I repeated to her what had happened that nightfall.

"Looking back to when it first appeared, that vision in my dream,
a figure in black and white diamond shapes, with a deadly scheme—
he grinned a wicked crooked smile with the evil he had planned.
He looked directly at me with his eyes, with a dagger in his hand."

My wife and I looked at each other and then to the man in the sleigh.
Was he the one who came in the dream? Was there any possible way?
Did that also mean he was the one who slew the others that day?
So, what were we to do, we asked with much concern and dismay.

We'll drop him in a hole in the ice, and that will take care of him.
We made that decision while knowing that the task ahead was grim.
We continued on with our wintry trek till we came upon the lake.
I gathered strength to steel myself for what I was about to undertake.

I halted the horses at its edge, took a sharp metal pole to poke,
chipping away at the ice till at last the remaining pieces broke
to reveal the rushing currents below to be his watery grave.
My wife was having second thoughts. *Was this any way to behave?*

I pulled the man out from the sleigh and dragged him along the ice.
I lowered him slowly into the cold water depths without thinking twice.
The current then took him immediately, and he was out of sight.
I stood by the hole and looked at the sky. Was my hindsight right?

Nothing was said for the rest of the trip as we traveled on and on.
We arrived back at our village home. All daylight by then had gone.
I started a fire to warm ourselves, but our thoughts kept silent
of all the things that had happened that day, one so very violent.

Some months passed by, but then a knock came upon our door.
Three soldiers in the local baron's colors, our reckoning in store.
The leader walked right into our home and stated he wanted to talk
of a missing man in diamond-patterned clothes that he was trying to stalk.

With a worried look, my wife drew back, thus fearing the very worst
as the leader took a seat and began to say the following to us first,
"The jester was a wanted man," he said. "Of that, make no mistake.
Someone saw you with such a man one day upon the lake."

He stared and asked me directly then, "Have you ever seen this man?"
"No," I lied. "We've been home ever since the winter storms began."

"That's a shame," he replied nonchalantly, "for the baron has offered a reward,
for anyone who may come forward—of course by their own accord—
may claim a purse of silver coins if they provide any further intel,
for he's wanted for killing the baron's bride-to-be and her parents as well."

I looked at my wife and she at me with excitement in our eyes—
thoughts of what that would mean to us, to receive such a rich prize.
So then I confessed and told him about what happened that fateful day,
how we'd come across that terrible sight of slain ones on the roadway

and also of finding the jester, too, and what came to me in my dream—
how we slid his body under the ice and of hearing his freezing scream.
He listened intently to all of it and said, "The baron will be most pleased.
He'll offer you a fine purse of silver coins, as he'll be very relieved.

"You must come with us now to his manor house,
with your story so you can tell
what you've just recounted for me to the baron,
and then it shall all be well."

I entered his home and stood before him sitting in a stately chair.
The baron slowly leaned forward, and with a piercing stare,
asked me just one question, "The jester is truly dead?"

I lowered my head and answered him. "Yes, my lord." I said.
He threw a fat purse full of coins on the floor, saying "Here is your reward.
Say nothing to anybody about that day, or I'll see you put to the sword."

When I reached home, I was very concerned by what had just occurred.
Was I am in some sort of plot? I thought. *Was I being guiltily lured?*
But my wife only saw shiny silver coins, and with a grin she said,
"Our lives have been enriched, husband—good times for us ahead."

In the months that passed by since then, our lives were very good.
Nothing more was discussed of the days on the lake, nor ever they would.
But then came that fateful day with a knock upon our door.
There stood soldiers of the king's royal guard, our reckoning perhaps therefore.

The captain walked right into our home and stated he wanted to talk
of a missing man in diamond-patterned clothes whom he was trying to stalk.
My wife drew back with a worried look as she feared the very worst
as the captain took a seat and began to say the following to us first.

"The jester was a wanted man," he said. "Of that make no mistake.
Someone had seen you with such a man one day upon the lake."
He stared and asked me directly then, "Have you ever seen that man?"
"No," I lied. "We've been home ever since the winter storms began."

I was worried about the baron and what he had cautioned me,
that if I spoke of it to anyone, death by sword his promise to be.
So I uttered not another word, my secret to keep inside
till the captain smirked and offered this as he leaned forward to confide.

"That's a shame," he nonchalantly said, "for the king has offered a reward
for anyone who may come forward—of course by their own accord—
may claim a purse of silver coins, if they provide any further intel,
for he's wanted for killing the baron's bride-to-be and her parents, as well."

I looked at my wife and she at me with excitement in her eyes
and thoughts of what that would mean to us to receive another sumptuous prize.
Then I confessed and told him about what happened that fateful day:
how we'd come across that terrible sight of slain ones on the roadway

and also of finding the jester, too, and of what came to me in my dream—
how we slid his body under the ice and heard his freezing scream.
He listened intently to all and said, "The king will be most pleased.
He'll offer you the fine purse of silver coins, as he'll be very relieved.

"You must come with us now to the castle
with your story, so you can tell
what you've just recounted for me to the king,
and then it shall all be well."

He insisted that I bring my wife along, so we followed in our sleigh
while thoughts of riches danced in our heads as we traveled on our way.

We arrived at the king's fortress, and were led in to the great hall
with tall marble columns and chandeliers—so many sights to enthrall.
We then bowed to the noble king as we anticipated a reward we knew.
He said, "The captain here has told me your tale. So tell me if it's true."

I said, "Yes, your royal highness, for what happened that day
is truly as I said, I swear. Those memories will never go away."
The king became serious as he asked, "So you killed the jester?"
"Only due to my dream vision," I said, "that told me he was the aggressor."

"Well," replied the king who looked right down at me, "You were wrong!
The jester was my jester," he shouted, "who wanted to tag along
with the lord and lady and their daughter on that fateful day,
and because of your reckless actions, his life he had to pay."

The king rose and commanded his guards to bring the baron in.
They dragged the poor man by his arms, and he repented his sin.
The king was disgusted by his sight with tension in the air
as he said, "You all are to blame for this, and therefore you all must share

"the punishment that will be dealt to you, for what you all have done.
Let me tell you now the true events that day, one by one.
Why do you think the baron gave you such a richly sum?
Because the jester was the only witness of the death that was to come.
The jester was an innocent man, and before freezing by the road,
carved in a tree what really happened, and his markings showed.

"It was the baron's soldiers that came and butchered those innocent ones.
He wouldn't marry the lord's daughter, so he silenced all their tongues."
To the baron, said the king, "My executioner will gladly remove your head."
Then to my wife and me, "You believed in a dream," he said.

"You thought of it only in literal terms, and that was a big mistake.
You have to know the difference between what is real and what is fake.
The jester was the only remaining one, and you took care of that.
Take them to the dungeon cells," he ordered, and then he spat.

So now my story brings us back right back to where I started,
and it's certainly not one—oh, no—not one for the faint-hearted.
For it was I whose actions had brought us, then,
to a woeful, damp cold cell
with the hanging noose awaiting us
when twelve chimes will ring from the bell.

The Bloodstone

The clouds had never moved away, and the night sky was unclear
as he sat alone thinking about his strange and difficult year.
He stared at the red-spotted green gemstone on his tabletop,
for he knew it was all he had to use to make his demons stop.

He rose and made his way across the room to look into the mirror,
and as he drew closer to it, ever nearer and nearer,
he saw the long gash upon his face, a constant reminder of the past.
He was aware and understood his fate not one he had asked,

for that night he had visited the fortune teller in the older section of town.
He had entered through a beaded curtain into a room dark brown.
She sat at her table lit by candlelight, the teller who was so renowned,
and as she cackled her spirit laugh, she placed her tarot cards down.

She gazed and sighed and was very silent without another sound,
till at last he asked her the question, "What is it that you have found?"
"This card represents a voyage of sorts that you must duly make.
This card represents conflict awaiting but is one you must undertake.

"This card tells me it will be upon the sea, so that would mean by ship.
This card represents a demon lurking, so be careful on your trip.
This card shows a wolf with one eye and a woman bound in chains.
The last card shows a stone you must give up to chase away your pains."

As he listened intently to what she said, he played with the bloodstone.
He felt uneasy anticipation of what lay ahead, with the vision she had shown.
He rose from the table, thanked her, and gave her coins of silver.
He knew what lay ahead would be, both unknown but familiar

as who are we to think that we have complete control of our lives
because only destiny will determine that for that is what destiny drives?
For a lifetime, one can strive, perhaps, and find life that duly thrives,
but there can be another path found as well, where one just barely survives.

That is where he found himself thinking only of what would be next.
He felt angry about what had happened to him. With emotions raw and vexed,
he returned then to his room at the inn to pack his meager supplies.
Memories filtered through his mind of a wolf and a woman's cries.

He held the bloodstone in his palm and remembered what had been told
as the tales all said it was the best gemstone always to have and hold.
If you want to recover your true self, that is the one they all say
to hold in your hand when fate does come on the judgment day.

He was determined to face his demons, and to prove it to himself,
he reached up and grabbed his scabbard to remove it from the shelf.
Attaching it securely to his belt and inserting his long-bladed sword,
he opened the door and stepped out, to the wharves he started toward.

The night air was much chillier, and then it began to sleet.
His walking cloak draped upon his shoulders as
he strode down the dim lit street.
No one else was about that night as he walked on silent and alone.
The only sounds came from alleyways where
drunkards slumbered and moaned

or stray dogs that rifled through the trash to find scraps of meat and bone.
He walked to his fate as he nervously rubbed his cherished, beautiful stone.
The bloodstone was his only solace, its meaning courage and strength.
And whatever path his future held, he would go to any length.

Those were all the thoughts he had as he walked toward the docks,
where ships anchor in calm waters sheltered by harbor rocks.
He inquired with each of their captains to see where they were bound
and convinced one with persuasion because that one came around.

He agreed to drop him near the place, the one they called Wolf Island.
But the crew would stay and remain on deck
yet would give him a helping hand
by providing a raft so he could make his own way to the shore
and would pick him up three days hence on their return, he swore.

Many tales have been told about it, that island of the wolves
and the demon spirits that emanate there like a magnet pulls
ships and men to their utter destruction. Such was said of that place,
and nothing was ever found of them who all vanished without a trace.

So the captain said, "If you're still alive and I see you on the shore,
I'll anchor our ship, and when you row back, we can hear what you've
learned of lore."
Both men agreed upon the terms and then up the gangplank he went
to the main deck as the ship moved out. He thought of what it meant.

He stood alone at the railing and stared into the blackness of the seas.
He remembered when it all began in the coolness of night breeze.
His friends and he had been young and foolish when they went to that place
to find themselves surrounded by wolves and that awful nightmare chase.

The wolves slyly divided them up to devour them one by one.
With no weapons to protect themselves, they were eventually outrun.
It was truly a haunting scene, one he could never forget
nor all that remained in those last few moments with their ultimate regret.

He and a young woman were all alone as the demon wolves crept closer,
the leader of their pack in front, the one you could call the imposer—
an exceptionally large grey wolf with one eye who offered a proposal
"to either accept or death it will be, for you're both at my disposal.

"This all depends upon you, young man, as the lady shall stay with us,
but I promise I will release her if you think you have the guts
to find me a mystical bloodstone and bring it back to me here.
And if you decide never to return or perhaps you just disappear,

"you may be free, but you'll never forget that you left her here alone
with a pack of demon wolves who'd enjoy a hearty meal of human bone."
With a slash of his claws, he cut the man's face deep, saying,
"This will be your reminder
to find exactly what I have asked for, and to also remember her."

The wolves all watched as he stumbled to the beach and rowed away in fright
of what had taken place on Wolf Island on that terrible, terrible night.
Perhaps you can understand the dilemma he found himself in.
What would be his final decision? For it was all up to him.

"Wolf Island is off the starboard bow," from the mast a sailor shouted out.
The young man standing beside the rowboat on deck cast away his doubt
and clambered in as they hoisted it down to settle on the waves
as the captain shouted down to him, "We'll see you in three days."

As he rowed away, he wondered if the wolf would honor his word
or was that just an impossible outcome, a result awfully absurd,
to trust that he and the woman would be free to just walk away
once he gave up the treasured bloodstone to the wolf all grey?

He pulled on the oars and guided his boat to the beach he saw before him.
He realized his chances somewhere between slim and grim,
but he was determined and fueled by the powers of the bloodstone.
His plan was set and decided upon with the outcome still unknown.

He beached his craft on to soft sand and climbed the rocky cliffs
then began to prepare the just deserts for the wolves, his deathly gifts:
metal snare traps placed on the ground and nets to swoop into trees
and deep holes with sharp wooden spikes covered up with leaves.

He raised his head and let out a howl to let them know he was there.
As the wolves came out, he taunted them, drawing them in to where
he began to run as fast as he could, the wolves chasing at his heels.
Then he heard his metal traps snapping and
listened to their cries and squeals.

Others became caught up in the nets, whipsawing them into midair,
the remainder fell into the pits with spikes,
and the wolves howled in despair.
And then a complete silence, but he hadn't yet seen the grey one,
so another challenge loomed ahead for him before it was all to be done.

As he climbed up to higher ground, he saw an opening for their den.
He entered cautiously with long sword drawn to meet the grey one again.
The large wolf with one eye sat on its haunches, the woman at his side.
It bared its large teeth as it said, "I thought you'd gone to hide."

"Are you foolish or smart," the wolf asked,
"to be standing here in front of me?
Did you bring me what I asked for, young man, as did we not agree?
For if not, then well, you're done for, but if you have it, perhaps we'll see."
The wolf then stared at him intensely while the woman wept silently.

The man reached into his pocket and pulled the bloodstone out.
Then placing it in his palm, showed the grey wolf, so there was no doubt.
The wolf leapt forward with lightning speed as the
man swept his long sword down,
slicing the head cleanly off the wolf's body, its blood spilling all around.

The dead wolf lay at his feet as the man helped the woman to rise,
terror and shock expressed on her face but relief showing in her eyes.
He consoled the terrified woman, and together they left the den,
although looking back nervously every now and then.

As they made their way back to the beach to sit on the sandy shore,
"Bless you, sir," she said. "For your return I've so long prayed for.
I didn't know if you would ever return. My death would surely be.
But why didn't you just give him the stone, for wasn't that the guarantee?"

He replied, "I couldn't trust the wolf, m'lady, and
the stone means a lot to me."
And as he gazed out over the clear blue waters, he finally began to see.
Looking down at the bloodstone in his palm,
remembering what had been told,
if you want to recover your true self, that was the gemstone to hold.
He realized then that the tales were true, and that is the one they all say,
to hold in your hand when fate does come on a judgment day.

With the sun slowly going down, he finally felt so completely free,
just her and him sitting on the sand with a beautiful sunset to see.
For the bloodstone had been his only solace,
bringing him courage and strength,
and the time had come, he realized, stretching his palm out at arm's length.

He knew that he was ready just to let his precious bloodstone fly,
confirming long-lasting peace for him. To it he willingly said goodbye
and threw it high out into the deep sea waters with a grateful sigh.
He looked up with only comforting thoughts and stared at the sky.

My Blue-Eyed Lady

I had a dream over and over,
of a young woman in a field of clover
along the coast by the cliffs of Dover.
She traveled alone, an eternal rover.

She came just appearing out of the mist.
Is she only a vision, or does she really exist?
And try as I might that dream to resist,
each night that vision did only persist.

She stood by castle ruins where the path ends,
and around her neck was a necklace of gems
and around her wrist, flowers tied by their stems.
A spyglass in her hand, she peered through the lens.

Shaded by branches of a tangerine tree,
what was she looking for, oh, so fervently?
I felt probing in my mind. Was she looking for me?
Suddenly I felt anxious, for how could that be?

Like cumulous clouds slowly rolling by
drifting continually along, up high in the sky,
perception and insight in my invisible third eye,
something inquiring closely, I could not deny,

Her blue eyes sought but did not find me yet.
Was it an innocent search or a veiled threat?
Each time I awoke, then, in a deep sweat,
but images remained, and I could not forget.

The visions continued, and night after night,
slipped into my subconscious, that visitant wight.
Blue eyes looked back at me through the sight
of her spyglass. She whispered, "It will be alright."

It seemed reacquaintance from longtime passed
or perhaps déjà vu that does ever last.
"What's happening here?" to myself I asked,
then garnered my strength for a question to ask.

I whispered back to her, "What is your name?"
She said, "You knew me before. It's still the same.
Our lives reincarnated from whence we came."
Was my mind playing tricks? Was it all a game?

She said, "When you see me, you will know it's true,
for it's not from this life's past that you knew.
It's many previous lives that we went through.
and our souls stay connected for me and for you."

Determined to seek, if there was truth to it
or just a result of a preordained minute
in my mind, I asked, "Where can we meet?"
She replied, "At the castle ruins, but be discreet".

I arrived at the cliffs along the seacoast,
would she be there, or was she a ghost?
"Castle ruins this way," read the signpost.
To the tangerine tree I went first and foremost.

I sat with my back up against a stone wall
as the sun went down, soon to be nightfall.
I stared at the sea and felt small,
needing resolution once and for all.

Was I so foolish to believe in a dream?
Had my mind taken it all to the extreme?
No one would appear now, it would seem.
So, I prayed to the Almighty, the one supreme.

"Tell me, Lord, what does this all mean?"
A vision in my mind came with this scene,
two angels with wings, the woman between
and wearing the necklace with gems of green.

I opened my eyes to see my mystical whisperer.
There was something familiar, but I didn't know her.
She held incense in her hands smelling of myrrh.
She approached then and said, "Evening, good sir."

Her fingers brushed strands of hair from her eyes,
and the way she did it seemed to hypnotize.
I was enthralled and bewitched by her blue eyes.
There was something about her I did recognize,

but how can I say that, as I'd never seen her before?
Because of simple things that you sometimes adore,
those memories you keep, deep down in your core.
I acknowledged that we two, we did seem meant for.

I took her hand and said, "I'll love you always."
She fixated me then with her blue-eye gaze
and said, "In all pasts and all futures, years and days,
our souls are connected, and that always stays,

"for when this life ends, we'll meet in the next.
We'll find a way to each other to reconnect."
I knew then in my heart and in introspect,
she was truly the one, nothing more to expect.

I took her hand in mine as we left that place—
my blue-eyed lady, one so full of grace,
my whole being fulfilled in a warm embrace.
She said this to me as I gazed at her face,

"We've always been together, forever, you see,
and that is just how it is supposed to be.
Forever and ever, through eternity—
one life at a time for you and for me."

Acknowledgments

Much gratitude to my initial readers who read every story I have written during the last two years. I thank Sylvia Nye, Cynthia Custeau, and my wife, Nancy, for your encouragement and support. I am also grateful for enthusiastic responses from Janet Gorth, Betty Lou Guilford, Carrie Kusza, and many others who kept my motivation at a peak. Special thanks to Mike Bendinelli for his thoughtful insight and advice.

My appreciation to Cynthia Crosson, an accomplished author in her own right, who first suggested I publish my stories and guided me in that endeavor, and last but not least, to Marcia Gagliardi, my editor and publisher, for helping me through the whole process.

Gary Wilson

About the Author

Canadian born Gary Wilson moved with his family to live in France for four years when he was young. He dropped out of college when he was twenty and backpacked throughout Europe. He lived with farmers in the mountains of Ketama, Morocco, worked on a kibbutz in Israel, slept on the beaches of the Mediterranean and rooftops of run-down hotels in Istanbul, Turkey. He traveled to thirty-three countries. In winters, he worked as an instructor at Killington, Vermont, where he taught more than a thousand people to ski.

He briefly attended the Art Institute of Boston and then exhibited his own work throughout New England. In 1980, he won the prestigious Emily Lowe award for contemporary painting at Allied Artists of

America in New York City. A slide catalog of the exhibit toured major US universities and then was archived in the Smithsonian Institution in Washington, DC. He was president of the Watertown Artists Association in a Boston suburb.

In 1989, married with children, he and his family moved to Whately, Massachusetts. He became finance manager for an international company, American Saw, with travel to Europe to visit customers and oversee their Netherlands operation. Years later, he worked supervising external audit firms for the eighth largest private company in the US, C&S Wholesale Grocers, before retiring in 2018.

He always missed what he felt was his purpose, creating art, as the realities of life interceded. He never resumed his painting and drawing after leaving Boston.

In March 2021, after his first shot for COVID-19, he began to experience verses in his mind at night. Somewhere between being awake and asleep, storylines crept. He has no idea where they came from, had never written stories before, and certainly had not written verse. Apparently, the vaccine boosted his creativity in a unique way, and it came not in paintings, but in words.

Visit garywilsonbooks.net.

Colophon

Text for *Moonlight Visions* is set in Adobe Garamond, a digital interpretation of the roman types of Claude Garamond and the italic types of Robert Granjon. Since its release in 1989, Adobe Garamond has become a typographic staple throughout the world of desktop typography and design. Adobe type designer Robert Slimbach has captured the beauty and balance of the original Garamond typefaces while creating a typeface family that offers all the advantages of a contemporary digital type family. With the introduction of OpenType font technology, Adobe Garamond has been reissued as a Pro type family that takes advantage of OpenType's advanced typographic capabilities.

Titles are set in Jazz font, the work of British designer Alan Meeks to capture the sophisticated elegance of the 1920s and 1930s. The bold roman style is enhanced with an interior design almost like a piano keyboard or the lit windows of a skyscraper.

www.ingramcontent.com/pod-product-compliance
Lightning Source LLC
Chambersburg PA
CBHW072355030726
47505CB00014B/1834